DEADLY BINGO

Tok Sort rephrased his questions. "If the nine of us were on a raft and the raft would sink unless one of us hopped overboard or was pushed overboard, would you do the shoving?"

"Such a corny example," Zeke sighed.

"Yeah?" Tok exploded. "Isn't that what colonist bingo is all about? Isn't it that we're too many on this little hunk of solar satellite of ours? What do you say, Soong?"

Soong looked across at him. "If you put it that way—yes," he answered softly. "I would also expect to be pushed overboard if I were the loser."

"And you, Zeke?"

"I don't buy your oversimplification."

"And you, Nobu?"

The guard grinned. "I'd push especially hard if you were the loser, sir."

"Why's that?" Tok asked icily.

"Because you invented the game. Sir."

syn • ec • tics (si nek tiks) n. (construed as sing.)
the study of creative processes, esp. as applied
to the solution of problems by a group of diverse
individuals.

—*Random House Dictionary
of the English Language*

Unisave

Axel Madsen

SF

ace books

A Division of Charter Communications Inc.
A GROSSET & DUNLAP COMPANY
360 Park Avenue South
New York, New York 10010

UNISAVE

Copyright © 1980 by Axel Madsen

An ACE Book

First Ace printing: February 1980

2 4 6 8 0 9 7 5 3 1
Manufactured in the United States of America

PART I

1

Tok Sort slipped into his robe. Without look-ing at Iyabo on the bed he crossed to the window and pushed the acclimatizer to high. He needed to put a measure of distance between himself and what she had just told him.

"You're mad or you're trying to blackmail me into something," he grinned incredulously.

"And tell me why you avoided Population Care, you of all people?" she asked from the bed.

"I just can't believe it." He inhaled a blast of recycled air.

"Nobody would." Her voice was sarcastic.

He pressed the button to make the curtain slide aside.

"Tell me it's some sort of eve-of-session prank," he said turning his back to her. The city and its white brilliance stretched to the domed horizon.

"Why should I kid you?" she asked in her ordinary scientist's voice.

He had an uncanny feeling of melted time, of finding himself ahead of where he was or should be. Below he saw the East River and the antique Queensboro Bridge in the shadow of the Long Island metal complexities. The city stretched south to Richmond, west to Des Moines and north to Quebec, but to the east it could only stretch to the last floating skyscrapers on the continental shelf. To look east was to imagine the nearness of the unconditioned sea.

"I just can't believe it," he said. His mind was totally crowded with this new experience.

"Happens every day," she said, factually.

"Sure, especially to Unisave delegates." He turned and looked at her. His feelings toward her were too complex to analyze.

"You must be the only closed-quota man who hasn't been restricted," she said.

Their eyes met. Ten minutes ago his first question had been how could it have happened. She had told him that after Tunde's death she had stopped capsulating. A split second later, he had realized it *could* be true.

"So why aren't you restricted?" she insisted.

"All sorts of dumb reasons," he conceded. "My appointment and transfer, a need to test the system, to feel above our own law." He probably was the only closed-quota man with live sperm in him. Iyabo and Misha Sev were women, Sal had made his own sterilization a media event, and the chairman and Zeke Dua were past the legal age, while Soong was an open quota. The rest of humanity was under the law.

"I'm hungry," she said, throwing the sheet aside.

It was nearly three hours since they had defied the scanners. His eyes followed her nude back and buttocks as she crossed to the dresser.

"And why are you thinking of keeping it?" he asked, logically. Her nudity was still too new not to disturb him.

"We aren't there yet." She wrapped a towel around her and faced him.

He saw hope and wanted to be effusive. "You must admit it's something of a mathematical near-impossibility," he smiled. "One in twenty-two billion."

"All conceptions are one in billions."

"One in twenty-two billion?"

He could see she was not amused. She picked up her clothes and walked toward the water-room. "Let's eat something upstairs," she said.

"Yes, we should be seen."

She slipped into the waterroom.

If he was honest, the very preposterousness of the whole thing had egged them on. The need to challenge moral and sexual taboos. This afternoon she had made him admit that the idea of doing it was exciting. They were inventing new ways of getting past the scanners at each other's apartment buildings although they had not yet dared to spend a night together.

He closed his eyes and breathed deeply before he dialed the acclimatizer down to medium and made the curtain slide back. The affair was shared imagination, shared experimentation and it had changed them. At this moment his own feelings were disorderly, strange and pre-mordial.

He heard her turn on the water and almost wanted to join her. They had never taken a shower together. And this was the first time he had turned around at the window before she had covered her nudity. Beauty was baffling. He had realized that one afternoon when she had fallen asleep for twenty minutes. His hand had traced the curves of her body under the sheet and he had imagined her skin black as UNCTAD people's pigmentation had been before homogenization. Progress might be cumulative, except in beauty. Iyabo's skin was that halftone darker that made him dream.

Tomorrow, their most controversial session would resume.

He got dressed. The colonies' proposal was powerful because it was simple and because it was ecologically appealing—to the third of the planet's population that was under sixty. Soong Ast's bingo would eliminate the geriatric excess. What had set off the debate seven weeks ago was not so much the fact that the colonies would be exempt—after all there was no geriatric overload in space—but Ast's rejoinder that his proposal was essentially just and fair. Zeke Dua had wondered out aloud where justice was if a sixty-year-old could lose to his ninety-year-old progenitor and Iyabo had said certain ecosystems needed their sixty-year-olds more than their hundred-and-twenty-year-olds.

Iyabo came out of the waterroom neatly dressed in her delegate's uniform and with a yellow scarf around her Nefertiti neck. He also slipped into his uniform and they stood in front of the mirror for an awkward moment, two tall and slim figures with modern, homogenized traits.

"No regrets," he said. The two words were midway between an affirmation and a question, although he hadn't intended it that way.

"And you?" she asked.

"Only in the sense of self-preservation," he smiled into the mirror. He wanted to be himself.

"I must concede you that, I guess."

"That goes for both of us. We both have to face tomorrow."

"All the arguments are on your side," she smiled with a twinge of irony in her voice.

"The arguments are on the side of self-preservation," he said softly. He moved close behind her and put his arms around her waist.

"It's odd to realize you can feel alone," she said.

"That you can want to be alone?" he asked.

Their eyes met in the reflecting glass.

"Something like that."

To be alone was antisynergetic and perverse, like watching the nudity of someone of the opposite sex. To be alone was antisocial and, like their liaison, innately unstable. Synergy ruled the planet, logically, but he sensed that they both shied away from any creative resolution of their new situation. At least for now.

He wanted to ask if loneliness also made her think of Tunde, since it was less than a year ago that her husband died, but instead hugged her. He felt he needed the assurance of her body against his.

"Oh Tok," she whispered.

He felt vulnerable to ancient influences that a modern person shouldn't feel. They were a pair of trespassers of their own law. They were their own joke. He looked in the mirror again and saw that her eyes were closed. A tender smile played on her full lips but he was still confused.

Upstairs, they got the best delegates' table at the bay window and Tok ordered meat analog, telling Iyabo he needed something hearty after what she had told him. He winked but her eyes followed a drive ship gliding down from the metal sky. The steel and chronium complexities covered the eastern half of the continent and busy billions lived under the metal skin and deep into the earth. There was no green to be seen, no soil, no life other than man. Up here there was little traffic, however. A few pleasure craft lazed against the iridescent dome sky. Slowly, the decelerating ship disappeared behind the structures on the Jersey side.

They started out with texturized carrot salad and were interrupted by autograph hunters. After they had both signed a dozen napkins and UN programs, Tok had a guard set up a privacy screen. He felt better. Iyabo wasn't sure. She was entitled to her moment of reverie, she was even entitled to her quota when it came right down to it, but she wasn't sure. That was the point. The six weeks' recess had been a tonic. He had seen Kikki and the children in Paris and had come back early enough to spend this short week with Iyabo.

"You are beautiful," he said.

She looked across at him and he watched her aquiline nose and severe brow, her high cheekbones, deep brown eyes and the yellow scarf that gave her skin a glow of amber.

"That's why I may want to keep it," she said, holding his gaze.

He had thought it settled—without words, as among civilized people, that she would do what any woman did in similar circumstances.

"But you know it is not possible," he said quietly.

"We can buy you a quota," she smiled.

He could see she was realizing both the theoretical correctness and the total absurdity of what she was saying.

"I can already see the scanlines," he grinned, pretending to play along. "I mean, TOK SORT IS PENALTY FATHER." He could see the capital letters dance across the video and the anchorperson tell the world he was trying to escape the rule he had helped make universal law.

Iyabo looked across at him. "Still, I have my right," she said calmly.

They ordered dessert. He didn't want to become angry, didn't want to argue and haggle because it made him small and ungenerous and hurt them both. Instead, he said he was innocent. "If you had told me, I would have had myself restricted," he said, meaning that if he had known she was decapsulated he would have dashed to the nearest Population Care center.

When the reconstituted fruit arrived, he looked across at her and quietly asked her why.

"I'm lonely," she answered, holding a spoonful of pear analog in midair.

"How can you say that?"

"Biologically lonely."

If the liaison was discovered it could be explained—the two of them working elbow to elbow for so long; she a widow, he a man too often absent from home, growing apart from his mate in an honorable way. But offspring? Like everyone else she had the right to replace herself, but claiming the quota was of unknown father carried its own social stigma. Naming him the penalty father was simply unthinkable. They would face an angry world. It would be a hundred video cameras staring them down as they tried to justify themselves. They would try to appear brave and overplay their courage. And billions watching would feel betrayed. Afterwards they would always hurry to escape hostile stares, forever hoping to go unrecognized.

He signed for the food. Widowhood did things to people, he thought. Tunde and Iyabo had been childless, had devoted themselves to genetics and seen their work rewarded with a joint Nobel prize. Tok sensed he was not yet at the core of her reason.

"Why?" he asked again with all the sincerity he could muster.

"Oh Tok, please."

"No really. Why?"

"Perhaps to buy back my vote." She seemed to look right through him.

He suppressed a sigh of relief. Downstairs while she was getting dressed, it had occurred to him that she had voted for gericide six weeks ago to get back at him and his quantitative arguments. But that was before. "If that's the reason," he said quietly, "my apologies should suffice."

"Don't overestimate your persuasive powers. I might have voted with the colonies for other reasons than your sarcasm."

They went back to his apartment and both called for messages. The Eurocom secretariat told him Sal Belem was due in at 2230 and that Zeke Dua was still meeting with President Hoo in Washington. Tok walked discreetly out of range of the visiplate as Iyabo dialed UNCTAD and told her staff she was leaving the UN penthouse restaurant shortly and was taking a ground car home. She was advised to watch the 2300 news if she was near a video as there were reports that Misha Sev had not yet left Moscow.

Tok watched Iyabo as she talked to her people on the screen and thought there were moments when he could almost bring himself to go through the shame and disgrace for her. Almost. He felt moved by the way she was all business with her staffers because he knew what was underneath her efficiency and beautiful Nobelized mind. Love was also complicity. It was sitting across from each other in the committeeroom and knowing their flesh had mingled and burned. Not as a joke on the others but as reason. Sometimes their relationship wasn't entirely real to him and sometimes, like now, he thought he understood everything.

When she was off the screen she went into the bedroom to get her things. He followed her and stood in the doorway. She looked at him and said, "Why? Because I have never had a child, because you're intelligent, because I have studied theoretical biology long enough."

She came across to him. "Theoretical biology gives you a funny respect for life."

He sat a long while in his study after she had said, "I'll call you in the morning" and left. Neither of them had said the last word obviously. Nothing was final. Perhaps he could convince her. He smiled to himself. She had to admit that her sailing into the committeeroom nine months pregnant was a howl. Or maybe the world would love it. Mother Unisave!

Why was he trying to kid himself? The world wouldn't love it.

He had always marveled at the effect of the final Assembly ratification seven years ago. People with open quotas did their annual capsulating until they were ready and couples who had already had their two children went to Population Care centers to have themselves restricted—Kikki had done it after the birth of Ise—so they could continue normal lives. But a whole era had come to a soft, yawning end. Sex had been something of an obscenity since earthside humanity had passed twenty billion a century ago. Divorce had become delicate and bootleg births a social anathema. Was it because he was an historian that he saw the irony? Less than two hundred years ago people had still flayed away insatiably. Absolute license was always shortlived and inevitably followed by times when books were expurgated and fig leaves plastered back on statues. Goatish sexuality was associated with the corrupt and mercantile ecosystems of the past and everybody took today's rectitude for granted.

He thought of Ank and Ise growing into thinking human beings. What would Ank think of him as the world's only quota cheat? Ise was too little to understand but in a few years she would be another victim, ostracized in school. Ank would no longer ask him for autographs for his school chums.

Impulsively, he got up to dial Paris but stopped himself halfway to the phone. It was 0550 in Europe and even if Kikki woke Ank and Ise up they would look sleepy on the screen and repeat the things their mother would whisper in their ears. And Kikki might sense something if he called at this time of night. He promised himself to call in the morning.

He felt silly standing in the middle of the study. It was still early. He switched on the video. Iyabo's secretary had advised her to watch the 2300 news but here was a clip of Sal Belem's skyport arrival. The general's imposing profile and hawknose dominated the reporters pointing their remote camerapens at him.

"General Belem, do you feel excess population elimination will actually become law?" One reporter asked.

"We're for life," the big Brazilian beamed. "We're for the future, for what is coming, not what is fading away."

Tok slumped into a chair and watched. On the wallscreen, Sal pushed through the crowd behind his ubiquitous deputee, Nilo. Belem stopped and allowed the reporters to focus on him. Vain bastard, Tok thought appreciatively. He'd have done the same himself.

The newspeople's questions came hard and fast. The general was asked whether he expected a lengthy debate or whether the Seven already had a concensus.

"Unisave's decisions are always metadetermined," Sal answered deftly.

He was asked if he didn't agree that longevity threatened the well-being of everybody and he answered that life was more precious than demographics. He was asked his reaction to joykillings and answered that such random murder of seniors pointed up the lack of world consensus, that geriatric sanitation was a sensitive issue.

"So is the deterioration of life because seniors live too long?" someone interjected.

"Which is why we're addressing ourselves to the question with an open mind," Sal said forcefully. "Synergy *will* be achieved."

In UNspeak, a bearded reporter asked the general to confirm that Delphic polls in his system suggested the terminally ill wouldn't mind volunteering for euthanasia.

Sal grinned. "Delphic polls tell people what they must *expect* of themselves. Terminal cases can't exactly anticipate their future."

The reply drew a chuckle or two from the reporters closest to Belem. Seriously, he added that voluntary euthanasia by the terminally ill wouldn't mean much, statistically speaking, since there were so few. Organ replacement and now organ regeneration kept lowering death-rates everywhere.

Tok thought his colleague looked great, brimming with vitality and confidence. The general was also wearing a new, tailored uniform. Of the seven of them, Belem was the oddest choice. The rest of them came from related fields—theoretical biology like Iyabo, demography, gynecology, past-interpretation like himself, or, in Jammu's case, a long, distinguished career in the UN.

Gericide was on all lips. Gags about bingo games and sanitary population flushing were as numerous as mass rallies by seniors and counterrallies by younger people who saw their immediate future diminished. There were jokes about the poor Grecicist who had coined 'gericide' for the proposed elimination of the excess old. Geron, gerontos-old man: shouldn't it be gerontocide? Gericide had stuck.

"The *absence* of consensus, the extraordinary absence of consensus is what makes this new session so fateful," Sal said.

A woman reporter asked if gericide didn't put the heaviest penalty on the most progressive regions, on those, precisely, who had crowned their upward thrust with longevity. Sal seemed to speak only to her when he answered that the

Southcone believed in progress like everybody else, but that the hemisphere hadn't lost touch with fate or compassion.

The first reporter was back, asking if Belem approved of the principle of gericide.

"All facts are not created equal," Sal parried lightly.

"There have been so many stories about your disagreements," someone tried. "Are most of them true?"

"Of course not, but that makes no difference. Nobody is interested in whether they're true or not."

"Can you confirm that you and Iyabo Att voted with the colonies?"

"Eurovision will invent any story and take pleasure in seeing it beamed to the colonies."

Tok smiled at his wallscreen. That was a cheap shot but not entirely incorrect. Actually, Eurocom columnists had come pretty close to guessing who had voted how six weeks ago, but none of the networks had hit bull's eye on the nature of the motion. Misha had proposed voluntary elimination of chronically ill seniors and Sal suggested voluntary euthanasia be extended to all terminal cases regardless of age. But all they had voted on, 4-3, was to continue discussions of qualitative measures. Nothing more. To Soong Ast's contention that if all men were equal, two lives were worth the double of one, Tok had joked that a sixty-year-old man might also be said to be worth the double of a hundred and twenty-year-old.

On the screen, the woman reporter asked the general what Unisave would do if a consensus could not be found.

"We'll keep trying," Sal beamed. "Nothing is hopeless. The colonies are pouring new energies into new knowledge and here on the planet we're constantly broadening social and spiritual horizons."

The reporters weren't satisfied, but Sal merely quoted chairman Jammu Nagpur that Unisave's mission was to save the planet, not to like or dislike principles.

A senior reporter with a twenty-first century accent asked point blank if gericide wasn't the inevitable future.

"There are many possible futures, all of them equally possible, if you accept the right assumptions," Sal answered, adding a touch that Tok thought pretty clever. With a theatrical gesture, the general asked the reporters what they *expected* him to say. The mediapeople had not been asked to think but to get General Belem on video. During the second they hesitated, Sal and Nilo slid away to the waiting hover.

"And that was the arrival of the Southcone's General Belem for tomorrow's Unisave session," the anchorperson cued in as the skyport scene faded. "In a moment we will have a commentary by Gil Por."

Tok cut off the video before any Gil Por could comment on anything. Instead, he found a classical audio channel and filled the room with what he was ninety percent sure was Mozart's Concerto No. 21. If there was one thing he loathed it was network commentators' cheerful assumption that everything could be reduced to their level.

He thought Sal did pretty well for a man trained in civil warfare and not in media fencing.

The genius of their Unisave law was, as the reporter had intimated, that it assimilated up*wards*, that a zero growth had meant a higher standard of living everywhere. Until homogenization, the history of contact between advanced and backward societies had been a sorry one. As anyone could see in hindsight, the melting of the races had been as beneficial as Ultraintelligent Computers, or UICs. The inhabitants of the old United States and the old Brazil had been the first to realize that integration would ultimately make them nations of light-brown people. They had recognized the obvious pressures that would make this happen, but they hadn't foreseen that with homogenization and UICs nation-states would also dissolve. As Jammu said, the Unisave law worked in the same progressive way. Even in the short hindsight of seven years, it was obvious that the law had lifted drag-behind ecosystems toward global standards. But gericide now threatened to reverse the upward spin. As the woman reporter had said, it would put the heaviest demographic penalty on those systems that had succeeded best.

Tok let the music carry him as he thought about procreation as a personal dilemma. The quota growing in Iyabo's womb was a one in twenty-two billion fluke. Every coming together of sperm and ovum was a chance encounter, as Iyabo had said; if not one in twenty-two billion at least one in two billion. Kikki and he had never separated, never had a need to. He lived here most of the time and she and the children stayed in Paris. Fidelity had been a matter of taste for them, a matter of being like everyone else.

Eurocom wouldn't like it if he pressed for divorce, but he could probably survive the scandal. What he couldn't survive was penalty fatherhood.

The quota was irreducible.

His mind slid into imaginary scenarios. Iyabo *was* pulling his leg; she was testing him, trying to find his threshold of endurance. Kikki was dying in a subsonic crash. He had never married; he had, but Iyabo was Kikki. Although that couldn't be. Iyabo's skin was that tone darker, glistening and, when they were lying together afterwards, it had a scent of long ago. Only Sal with his jungle warfare experience could have said he was just as awed by the immensity of man's past as by the future out there in the tin can habitats where Soong Ast and sixty million others were building the grand tomorrow and saying no one had to be a loser. He imagined he had had himself restricted like every other closed-quota man on earth and in the colonies. To Iyabo and him, the affair was neither desperate nor crazy. To the two of them, the affair was already a familiar game, already familiar gestures. He saw her naked again; he felt her mouth, the surrender of her thighs. To love a woman who was not your wife was archaic and perverse. Socially, it was reprehensible because it was self-centered and because it was so immensely private. And in a beehive, egotism and privacy were unnatural acts. Had to be.

But he was sure nobody knew, precisely because it *was* unthinkable.

2

Patel Nobu hurried down toward the front of the auditorium, nodding apologetically toward Professor Las.

"Eventually if you keep heating things up something else happens," the teacher continued.

Patel spotted an empty seat next to a girl in a red sweater.

"At great heat, the movement of hydrogen molecules becomes so violent that they start smashing themselves into electronically charged ions, and that, as we know, is the door to the fourth estate of matter."

Patel slipped down on the empty seat and turned on his recorder.

"Fusion is one of nature's more elegant tricks."

The needle on Patel's recorder danced with the teacher's words.

"Some molecules need less heat than others to ionize, but the phenomenon usually doesn't begin until five thousand degrees and that's not going full blast. At one hundred thousand degrees things start to happen, but, as you all know, heating hydrogen gases to sixty million degrees is just the threshold of plasma physics."

The class was only worth two hundred immigration units, but Patel thought old Las was just great.

"Plasma pervades the universe in various degrees of concentration. Plasma is the raw material of the stars."

The teacher glanced out over the evening class and repeated himself for the stragglers. His recap was accompanied by a rerun of the audiovisuals and Patel realized he hadn't missed anything. He looked at the girl he was sitting next to. She was pretty.

"Nuclear power for ships is routine," Las lectured, strolling in and out of the audiovisual projects of Noah's Ark ships. "But as we know, nuclear propulsion is not enough for any grand tour of the galaxy."

Patel felt his spine tingle as he listened to old Las. Two Thursdays ago it had been mercury usage as reaction mass to convert old ion drive ships. Last week, it had been matter transmission and time distortion, with audiovisuals of the new arks. Now, the teacher described the stupendous energies released by matter being heated to a hundred million degrees. The problem was not so much to find ways of heating up things as to contain such superhot matter. The most logical way of containing plasma was to spin it, "just as the universe does."

Somebody in the front row asked what the next generation of plasma-powered ships would look like, and Las obliged on the old visualizer. Such ships, he said as his doodles were projected on the screen, would have to be put in orbit before ignition because their rear nozzle spew of energy was the equivalent of a thousand nuclear explosions.

Patel had been five minutes late because he had wanted his boots shined and had looked for a shine-o-mat on four levels of Flushing station.

Old Javan was particular about uniforms on opening days when the hallways were swarming with newspeople. Maybe Javan would put a couple of extra men on tomorrow.

On the visualizer, Las drew strange architectural shapes and explained that deep space probers invented such structures during prolonged states of nongravity. The shapes were fragile and delicate as dreams and reminded Patel of the art he had seen on the torus. Las made the geometric forms turn on invisible axles and the computer visualized the no-gravity architecture from surprising angles. It was like that. Patel remembered his first docking, the tip of the huge solar mirror floating by the viewport, the colony itself below as they eased down to the hub of the giant bicycle wheel. Just before his body sagged under the retro deceleration, earth had come into view, cradle of mankind and cage for too many, nearly half a million kilometers away. He had felt the exhilaration of escape. He remembered the formalities and the first ride in the gravitic elevator through the spokes, the first view of the tube with its residential space and agroareas. The windows with the view of black space and sharp pinpricks of starlight were divided into panels by the strengthening cables that appeared like the thin silver strands Las was enhancing on the visualizer. Patel couldn't wait to get out there again.

Las spent twenty minutes summing up plasma physics. Then he did something unusual. He digressed "to the topic of the day" and told the class they had in their midst someone who knew the Unisave Seven personally. "Patel Nobu, will you please stand up," the teacher smiled.

All eyes were on Patel as he got up.

"Patel was on a tin can for two years before joining the UN security force," Las announced.

He almost blushed.

"What was your orbit?"

"A two-to-one resonant orbit." He cleared his throat. "Four hundred and thirty thousand kilometers at the farthest point and two hundred and ten thousand at the closest point to earth, taking a bit less than two weeks per revolution."

"And dawn and sunset every ninety minutes?"

Patel smiled and nodded.

"A working tin can?"

"Carbon extracts from main-belt meteorites."

To the class Las explained that Patel was taking space drive classes to accumulate enough units to qualify for reenlistment. "What did you do, by the way?"

"Second in command on a utility tug."

"And on your return?"

He hesitated because what he really wanted was more a dream than a contingent event. "I'd like to qualify for next year's deep probe."

"Tell me, Patel," the teacher said with an intriguing smile, "do you think old geesers like me should be sanitized out of existence?"

"Not you, sir."

"You've heard of joykillings." The teacher's benevolent grin didn't change.

"Yes, but not all young people are like that."

"People in advanced ecosystems are beginning to live to be a hundred and fifty, average."

Patel wondered why Las wanted him to defend old people. There were too many of them, but he had nothing against them personally.

"It's a question that concerns us all," the teacher said.

"Chairman Nagpur says the population battle must be fought and won here." He wondered what the teacher was driving at.

"And do you find it just that the colonies exempt themselves?"

"Well, since they were never overpopulated."

But Las wasn't antagonistic. He taught night class physics for emigration exams because he believed in space himself. In his youth he had visited a construction shack and a powersat and in recent years attended conferences at the twin cylinders and he liked to reminisce about early space industrialization. Now, he said there was of course no way that the colonies could be a relief for a congested planet. But age, too, was a new frontier. To live to be a hundred and eighty or two hundred was to discover perspectives as new as those afforded deep space probers. "As we look at earth from a few thousand kilometers and see the thin film of soil and atmosphere and ocean that makes life possible, we are struck by the fact that we're a closed system, that the mushroom cloud of ever-aging seniors is pressing against us. But as we look at life like Vernon or Sarah Akhmanova, from the vantage point of a hundred and eighty-some, we also get a sense of wonder, a sense that the oceans flow through all of us, and through all lands. Sit down, Patel. Space is a profound experience, but so is extreme old age."

Las spent the last minutes of his lecture talking about the need for adventure and excitement, the sense of purpose and achievement that space had given everybody. The colonies had made man realize his civilization would not become debris of a defeated technology. Patel had felt something of this on his torus but had never been able to put it in words as old Las now did. Challenge and response, the teacher said, led to new ideas, and a new sense of beauty.

Patel took a ground car home. The taxi plunged into a tunnel and he sat back behind the driver's seat and felt the acceleration as they flashed forward along the thin line of light forming along the ground, twisting among other mass-drive tracks guiding other ground cars. His mind was full of Lasian enthusiasm. Maybe he should explain all this to the chairman.

He was on permanent Unisave duty because of Jammu Nagpur; he knew that. The chairman had surprised him reading a textbook and they had started to talk. A couple of days later the chairman had told him he could read during sessions. Javan insisted that guards on fourth power committees stand or sit at the door of the committeeroom they were assigned to. Committee members never paid attention to guards and there was no rule against reading once a session was under way. You don't have to pretend to be interested in what's going on, Javan had barked at graduation, but you're expected to be alert.

Jammu Nagpur was a civilized person. Patel was sure no one would attack the Unisave chairman, or any of the other six, for that matter. It was difficult to get into the old UN tower, let alone up to the nineteenth floor. But guards were there for that million-in-one chance that some pervert with a grudge would make it into the room and spray death among the delegates. To earn his pay in good conscience, he had formed the habit of tilting his chair on its hind legs and putting it against the door. That way he could read and do his job at the same time. An aggressor would have to knock him over before he could storm into the committeeroom.

He leaned forward against the deceleration as the taxi crawled back up to ground level. No one objected to his studying, not even secretaries. How could they? They were rotated so often. Committee secretaries were smart-ass technopols, people thinking they were somebody because they knew how to summarize one meeting into minutes and read these minutes aloud at the beginning of the next. No thank you.

He let himself into his apartment. He would be twenty-eight and of age next month. Next Thursday he would come early and try to sit next to the girl again. She looked like she was his age, which meant they would be entitled to go off inhibitors together. Older guys on his cartwheel in space had told him sex was sensational at low gravity.

He put his blue uniform out on the chair. It was still in the cleaner's plastic. He took his service laser from the code-locked drawer and put it in the holster. His boots looked great polished like that. He wondered whether men aboard deep probes were armed. Colonies weren't. Would a captain of a plasma ship carry a laser? There sure wasn't anything out there that a dumb laser could settle.

He was working hard to get his units so he could apply for immigration status. If he could help it, he sure wasn't going to be earthsided with the crowds for the rest of his life. He was deft with a utility tug. He could cartwheel his little vessel and waft it into dock position like nothing. When he and Vassily tended rotating solar mirrors, they sometimes retrothrusted seconds before the huge panels swept past. To cartwheel through solar panels with the colony hanging below and to use the panels as vectors for swinging around the hull were standard jokes to give newcomers coronaries. A guy replacing solar cells once floated into a mirror and disintegrated.

He had never had "island fever," never requested rest-and-rehabilitation back here. It was earthsiders who made jokes about watching the sun come and go every ninety minutes. The two million colonists on his industrial habitat saw themselves as the first humans to really glimpse the possibilities and the prospects of the future. They thought of their colony as one small, bright island of hope. His own dream of course was to become a deep probe pilot.

He slung the belt over the back of the chair. It looked neat. Maybe he could tell the chairman to just hang in there. Then, if one day he was reading very deliberately and the chairman asked how his studies were going, he could say that salvation was in plasma physics, in the handling of very hot gases in magnetic fields. Jammu Nagpur would smile and maybe ask him to explain. Sometimes the chairman stayed after sessions, sitting in his chair above the horseshoe with his hands folded over his face.

3

"Since way back the idea of genetics has been to make man into superman," Zeke Dua observed politely.

"Man is still far from shared godhood, you must admit." Ro Twer reached for the sweetener.

"I'm a physician." Zeke remained standing at the end of the twentieth-century couch. He regretted that he had let himself be talked into spending the night at the White House and consoled himself with a second cup of espresso. His only vice.

"What counts most for a scientist, the quality of your choice or the objective you're pursuing?" the Secretary of State goaded.

"Both."

Mrs. Twer held out a demi-tasse for her husband.

"Maybe it was the quality of the initial choice," Twer smiled.

Zeke carefully balanced his cup and remained standing. "I'm not a geneticist."

"But your colleague is."

"Iyabo Att never worked in bioengineering, as far as I know."

"But she voted with the colonist."

For a second Zeke wondered how Twer could know. "There has been a lot of speculation about that vote," he smiled.

But the Secretary had had his little triumph and became jovial again. He sat back on the couch, accepted the coffee cup from his wife and said that whether superman was being bioengineered or not, scientists hadn't perhaps been as successful as people might have been entitled to hope they would be.

"Give us another million years," Zeke said, stirring a reconstituted lemon peel in his demitasse.

"Another million years!" Twer exclaimed in mock incredulity.

Zeke tasted his coffee. It was perfect, black and licorice sweet.

"You've had center stage for centuries now," the Secretary continued.

Zeke wanted to get to the point and let his glance drift to President Hoo and Nasiba Riss talking quietly by the old french windows. The First Lady was coming toward them and Mrs. Twer moved closer to her husband to leave a seat for her.

"There's still too much pain," Twer sighed. "Many people live meaningless lives."

Zeke smiled. "I didn't know science was also supposed to give meaning to people's lives."

Flo Hoo sat down on the armlean of the couch across from the Secretary and his wife. Zeke thought the First Lady looked pretty in her old-fashioned way. She wore a flowing dress that accentuated her fondness for the past. "A lovely dinner," he said with a little bow toward her.

"I'm so glad you're staying the night," she smiled graciously.

"I'm honored." Was giving in to flattery the ransom of being more famous than your host?

"You will be sleeping in the West Wing guest suite," Mrs. Twer said, to show she knew the White House.

"It'll be an early working breakfast," Twer winked as if to warn Zeke not to get too comfortable.

The President and the Secretary for Demographics approached. With the enlarged audience, Twer neatly picked up the conversation several speeches back, in effect telling Hoo that their Unisave representative didn't think too highly of the political process but had limitless faith in science.

"We were talking about the diminishing returns of vertical institutions," Zeke corrected. Politics was a raw nerve in this ancient municipality.

Hoo sat down next to his wife, saying government by politicians hadn't been all bad. "By the nature of things, a politician knows people and has a sense of popular aspirations and popular moods. With all due respect, people like you, Zeke, believe there are answers to everything in synectics."

"By definition, symbiosis is the association of two dissimilar organisms when it is mutually beneficial."

"The modern world is leaderless."

"In the old sense of the word, yes, Mr. President. And so what?"

"Perhaps people need a sense of direction."

"The colonies give us that."

"By proxy."

"In the past, too, most people lived great adventures by proxy. How many were with Columbus when he sailed west? How many with the first astronauts?"

Hoo smiled. "The twentieth century had leaders."

"Who thought thermonuclear war was the gravest issue when the real threat was growth."

"Still they didn't make war. Isn't that leadership?"

This was Washington, Zeke told himself. Stopping off here was like visiting Versailles or Stonehenge. Over dinner, the President had extolled the virtues of the free market system until the First Lady had tactfully reminded him of the fact that by the twenty-first century the free market had become too extravagant for a planet with finite resources, a planet just saved in the nick of time when powersats solved its energy needs. This was all *before*—before UICs could program themselves, before people's lives became rich and long, before Delphic polls, before horizontal interaction and creative synectics, before goals parliaments and ethics courts.

The nuclear standoff had not been statesmanship, but a medieval guessing game with theological overtones. It was not only what the Americans believed the Russians believed, but what the Americans believed the Russians believed the *Americans* believed. Hoo and Twer conveniently forgot that political institutions had been their own abstraction for two hundred years, that people had lost faith in the process when they lost faith in governments' ability to influence events. The twentieth century had not been the imperial golden age Hoo liked to remember, but the century of parochialism and of ethnic tribalism. The twentieth century was the Middle Ages when power moved from above and, during brief revolutionary upheavals, from below, instead of horizontally as in the modern world. Today's UN was not nationalism multiplied by a couple of hundred nation-states; it was not world government but world symbiosis. And ecosystems were not neat overlays of former countries. Homogenization, which had made everybody look like premordial Hawaiians, had erased tribalism and the colonies had given a merged humanity a focus and a future. Unisave and Unido and the other symbiotic agencies didn't make laws. They managed consensus.

"And it attracted the best people," Twer said.

"Because public office was rewarding, exactly," the President acknowledged.

Zeke didn't listen. His mind was back on Misha. He had barely landed from Los Angeles before one of Twer's aides had told him Misha Sev had been replaced. On the way in, Twer had come up with several limp hypotheses. Yet why *was* she being replaced?

Zeke watched the portrait of one of the Imperial Presidents while he listened to Hoo and Twer talk about the glories of party politics. Zeke sneaked a peek at his digit and put down his demi-tasse with emphasis. If Hoo and his cabinet wanted any input this was the moment. "To get back to the upcoming session," he coughed.

"Yes," Riss said immediately.

Zeke liked the prim Secretary for Demography. She had keen eyes and lived in the present.

Nasiba Riss outlined the administration's final suggestions in a few short phrases. Looking from the President to Twer, to the First Lady and the standing Zeke, she said the municipality believed gericide *could* be defeated. Did Dua think he could convince his colleagues to agree to the euthanasia of all persons reaching sixty one year rather than all colonial lottery losers over sixty? she asked. If, instead of eliminating one third of all persons sixty and over, Unisave started the program with one specific year's crop of sixty-year-olds, the number of people involved would be so little as to be demographically insignificant.

"I had in mind a slightly different approach," Zeke interrupted.

"But do you think Unisave is open to persuasion?" Hoo asked.

"The recess may have altered both pro and con positions," Zeke answered. "And the news that Moscom is replacing Misha Sev adds an extra dimension of uncertainty."

The President looked worried.

"What *is* your approach?" Nisiba asked.

"To suggest that we start in the other end, so to speak. Instead of beginning with sexagenarians, we start with all hundred-year-olds and over, followed the next year by one third of all ninety-nine-year-olds, then one third of all ninety-eight-year-olds."

"Nice," Hoo smiled.

But Nasiba objected that to wait a year meant the ninety-nine-year-olds would be centenarians and that if you had both ninety-nine and hundred-year-olds play colonial roulette the second year, you would in effect force the centenarians to play twice.

"But next year the surviving centenarians will be a hundred and one," he smiled.

"I'm sorry, it's only in the third year that it doesn't work."

Demographics was not his forte but he got her point that if in the third year you had all ninety-eight, ninety-nine and hundred-year-olds play, the second year's ninety-nine-year-olds would play a second time the following year as centenarians.

"It keeps getting worse as you go up the ladder," she explained. "If you start with sixty, by the time you're a hundred you'll have played for your life forty times."

"My point is to water down the principle of geriatric sanitation," Zeke said.

"The only way colonial bingo can work is to have people compete within their own age groups."

"Okay, but there are fewer hundred-year-olds than sixty-year-olds and to eliminate a third of the world's centenarians must mean a lesser bloodbath."

Nasiba agreed and he reiterated that the point was to make gericide demographically insignificant. To squash any premature hopes, however, he added that there was of course no guarantee he could pull it off.

"But four of you voted against Soong Ast six weeks ago," Twer interjected.

Zeke was getting impatient. "Six weeks ago, we voted, 4-3, to recess, not to kill the colonist proposal."

The Secretary of State slumped deeper into the antique couch.

Zeke assumed the Hoo cabinet took the California joykillings into account, but to be sure he asked Riss.

"You mean the youth rallies?" Twer asked.

"I mean youth gangs killing seniors for the thrill of it," Zeke said drily.

Hoo leaned forward and said his government

was very much aware of divided public opinion, which meant symbiosis seemed impossible. Twer asked if Zeke thought Unisave would consider postponing colonial crap shooting until "a logical one hundred years, or even a hundred and twenty?"

"People have all too easily adjusted to sixty," the First Lady smiled sadly.

"But today, sixty is your prime youth!" the Secretary insisted.

Nasiba let her eyes wander from face to face as she explained that people liked the symmetry. At thirty you replaced yourself, at sixty your children were thirty and you played colonial bingo.

In his crablike, sidestepped way, President Hoo said he tended to agree with her. To ask for a delay to a hundred meant starting out from a weak position, he said, launching into a little lecture on the politics of handling divisive issues.

Again Zeke thought the unspoken fact of the evening was that both he and the President were fifty-four and therefore less than six years from being potential bingo players themselves. Their generational complicity was clear in the way they listened to each other and, before dinner, in their exchange of glances while aides pored over position papers. Of course sixty was your prime youth. In the old days it had been different, but UICs had revolutionized medicine.

He watched Hoo. The President didn't look any older than himself, he thought. By modern measurements, Hoo was short and spare. He had an authority that was undeniable, an abrupt decisiveness that could catch you off balance. He sometimes gave a funny little shake of the head; quizzical, impatient, not expecting answers. He was not easy to like but he inspired confidence in a dogged, sly way. The supporters of this former Montreal judge said he had done more than anyone since Jefferson to lower the voices and the pretentions of politicians. To his detractors he was a sentimental relic of the past, faintly comic but perfectly harmless.

When Zeke listened again, Nasiba was saying that, ideally, increased longevity should make for a better planet by allowing selfless, wise persons to undertake complex new projects for the benefit of all.

"Who wants a world run by vigorous centenarians?" Hoo smiled.

Zeke could think of Sarah Akhmanova as someone with more ideas than many people a tenth her age. He had felt like a centenarian last night in front of the L.A. students. Speaking in the cavernous old Royce Hall had been bad enough, but he had expected sharper questions from the floor. Perhaps it was always like that when you returned to academia after a long absence; you expected *them* to be brighter. He thought of Misha's population cycle study. Her book went all the way back to Antiquity to show that people's attitude toward their elders had always been ambivalent at best; downright cruel at worst. The hatred of the old was nothing new; their number was.

"The noblest role of age is an affirmative one," Hoo reflected.

"You're getting too deep, Dal," his wife interrupted gently.

"The ultimate affirmation of living is to know

how to die," the President insisted.

Zeke looked at his digit and said he had a long day ahead of him. He had felt a need to meet Hoo but the detour, he now realized, had been in vain. He should have known that no fresh ideas could come from an obsolete decision-making system.

Twenty minutes later he was in the West Wing guest suite on the phone with Tina. She was in her white terrycloth bathrobe. He told her his room was a museum piece and turned the phone so she could see.

"How was the dinner?"

"It was one of those everybody-relax-sit-down affairs."

"Anybody there?"

He knew what she meant. "No. Twer and wife, Nasiba, aides."

"I thought you said that was for tomorrow morning."

"That's why I'm staying over, the working breakfast." He didn't want to get into details for fear he'd tell her how futile this whole Washington detour was. Instead, he told her about the food—risotto milanese and fettucine with reconstituted minced onions. To please her, he added that Flo Hoo had worn a flowing zebra dress that made her look like an old-style candle. "I almost wanted to light her up."

Tina scrutinized his face as she did when she was concerned about his physical wellbeing. "You look tired, Zeke," she said. "Try to get a good night's sleep."

"Yes, I didn't sleep much in L.A. last night."

"I don't know why you let yourself be talked into those silly things."

He mentioned there were strong indications Misha was being replaced, which made Tina remember that Tok Sort had called.

"See you in the morning, darling," he said and blew her a kiss. A minute later he dialed Tok and saw him sitting in his living room in his evening uniform with classical music blaring.

"Nineteenth century, I bet," Zeke smiled.

"No, Mozart."

Neither of them had any good theory as to why Misha was being replaced by this Bo Lim, now scheduled to sky in at 0630.

"That is, except replacing an older representative with a younger one," Zeke said. "It looks smart, and now only Jammu and I are embarrassingly close to the big six-o."

"I hadn't thought of that," Tok admitted, adding that to him the surprise appointment was probably nothing more than a smokescreen to camouflage Moscom's lack of ideas.

"I'll buy that except for the eleventh hour appointment."

"Okay, but that also kills your old age theory. If Moscom wants to ease out the old girl and have a bright kid in the seat, why wait until the last minute?"

That was true, too. "Demographics here tells me the new guy is a bioengineer."

Tok chewed on that for a moment. When he spoke his voice had become intriguing. "Maybe Moscom thinks the solution is in gene splicing."

The idea was a little too farfetched for Zeke's mind. Scientific advances rested on the foundation of painstaking methodology and orderly disclosures, not on diplomatic bluster. If Moscom bioengineers had made a breakthrough in

geriatrics, it would be revealed in other nerve
centers of the planetary synergy; Medplan if it
had to do with biology for example, Unido if the
genetic innovation had to do with food production. "No, I just think the guy is a bioengineer as
Iyabo is a biologist, you're a past-interpreter and
Soong and I are physicians," he said.

Tok told him his White House dinner had been
a filler item on the local 2300 news—"buried
under Sal's skyport interview." Zeke termed the
dinner "a social, once-over-lightly" affair and
Tok winked, wondering how social it could be
with Tina staying in Manhattan.

The Seven didn't socialize much but Tina continued to make valiant attempts at "thawing
them out," as she said. Her dinner parties
weren't too successful, no doubt because seven
people watching each other around the horseshoe every day weren't too eager to continue
around a dinner table at night. Still, their annual
weekends at the Montauk lighthouse were popular with the Seven and with their staffs.

"See you in the morning," Tok yawned.
"Maybe we should send some sort of message to
Misha, congratulating her or something, to smell
out this bioengineer."

"Don't worry, I'll *ask* him."

"Should be fun," Tok winked.

They hung up and Zeke felt forcefield elec-
tronics regulating thermostats, acclimatizers
and a hundred other environmental necessities.
But he could also smell mold and history. Tok
had once cracked a joke about pulling the plug
on the millions of wealthy people who had had
themselves deepfrozen before death and were
lying waiting, at minus four hundred centi-

grades, for a more enlightened century. If somebody pulled the plug here, this room would be
positively spooky. Now, the jokes weren't about
cryonics but about high-speed plastic surgery
among fifty-year-olds. Not that anybody thought
they could fool Population Care computers. The
idea was just to go to beehives unnoticed—and
unmolested. Youth gangs were on the rampage
in California, Estado del Norte, Djakarta, Rio,
Kiev and other beehive places. There were instances of reverse violence, too. One hundred-
and-ten-year-old visitor to Tokyo had gunned
down twenty-two teenagers with an ancient
raygun before he was subdued. Of course few
real seniors ventured into beehives these days.

Washington was not Tina's kind of place. It
was too artificial, too spooky, she said, like
Brasilia and Strasbourg, capitals created in
theory and left behind in newer perspectives.
Tina loved Manhattan. Ladies in their forties
loved contemporary city life and he loved
watching Tina love it. He thought the forties
were the age when women were most beautiful,
when they were beginning to be interesting,
even to themselves. Maybe that was the joke on
the millionaires in their cryonic suspension—
their children were living the life they had
dreamed of, living younger and longer on the
continuous swelling crest of medical triumphs.
At forty-seven, Tina looked like a girl of eighteen
of a century ago—she said he resembled video-
clips of his grandfather at twenty. And they were
promised at least another century and a half of
disease-free existence—two hundred years if
you were an optimist and thought of the dysfunctions being conquered right now. In their

second century, they wouldn't live in Manhattan—they wouldn't *want* to live in a beehive, but under a new dome in a new suncity on the continental shelf or in another system. A life of leisure and inner growth awaited them. Like other seniors they would discover vistas of human development that former centuries could only have had the dimmest awareness of.

The colonies beamed down inexhaustible energy from the powersats, Unido produced the biomass and the UN ruled a rich and varied planet with metadetermined synergy. Seniors had their input just as active age groups did, except in Unisave. That had been normal when the General Assembly created the agency in 2181. Unisave dealt with those few years in a person's life when he or she went off inhibitors, sought a mate and procreated, legally the age between thirty and forty-eight.

Which was the reason Moscom was trading down, he concluded and walked into the restored twentieth century waterroom. At his own appointment seven years ago, he had been forty-seven.

He thought of Tina. He had liked the four days in Oregon. She didn't travel with him very often but she had come to the western White House. He had told her the Hoos wouldn't be there, but that the President had let him have the ancient government enclave as a courtesy for a week.

The Oregon dunes had stunned them— stretches of sandblasted beach pines and hard sand you could almost walk on like thin ice, only to sink in to your ankles now and then. And the waves of the unconditioned ocean. He would give a fortune to be able to live in such a place—

not that there were any such places. Or would
he? You could go mad in all that premordial
serenity, that sky that wasn't weathercon-
ditioned, that eternal ocean. You could hear it
from the house at night. He had sat there on a
dune while Tina looked for driftwood and he
had watched the unconditioned sun sink into
the Pacific, coloring high clouds a long time
after it disappeared. Tina had come and curled
up with him. She hadn't been scared, just solemn and apprehensive like himself. A few
kilometers to the north and south of this forgotten piece of government property, highrisers
stretched to Juneau and to Santiago de Chile. It
was a kind of scenery that made you realize
profound things.

He was grateful to Hoo for having given him
the chance to experience what only a handful of
people ever had. Tina had skied back to Manhattan before the Berkeley think tank sessions.

No wonder medical students in the past had
shied away from gerontology. Until the UICs, the
study of old age was a depressing inquiry into
one long downhill slide. He had encountered the
ranker injustices of biology as an intern himself.
Back then they practiced euthanasia in their own
fashion—do-nothing euthanasia. A nurse called
and said the person in 4322 was having respira-
tory failure and you took your time. By the time
you got up there, it was all over in 4322. The next
step had been God Committees to determine
who should have vital organ transplants and
when newborns with birth defects should live.
What he had tried to tell Twer tonight was
perhaps that medical science had been stupefy-
ingly simple until Malthusian mathematics had

made medicine bite its own tail. Before Population Care, doctors concentrated on saving life; now they had to decide when to snuff it out.

In Berkeley, they had run the colonist figures backwards and forward and the projections had checked out. It had been refreshing to plunge into academic medicine, to see the latest wizardry in operating rooms, to feel the luxuriant hush of a surgical lounge and to be surrounded by sharp interns and followed by skeptical residents. He had almost taken the chief of surgery up on his invitation to jump into a scrub suit and do a round. But his area had been the susceptible conscience of the ultraintelligent computers and Dr. Fow and his crew at the terminal. They had come up with a couple of goodies which he would use tomorrow. If the one-quota-per-human-being Unisave rule of seven years ago wasn't enough to maintain absolute zero because people lived longer, the Berkeley calculations had pinpointed how minute the excess was. "Minute but growing," as Dr. Fow had grinned.

4

Soong Ast let a boyish smile play on his long, clever face as he entered the Hundred-Forty mission on the dot of 2330 and was shown directly to the library.

"One moment," the male secretary said and left.

The room had a high ceiling and a comfortable mixture of memory reels and premordial print media on tall shelves. He crossed to the window, conscious of the fact that some video eye might be on him. Below, the lanes of ground cars glided into new patterns and to the right he saw the antique Golden Arch and East St. Louis beyond. His driver had told him the north-south ground car axis ran along the bed of an ancient river. During his two years on earth he had never been this far west in Manhattan. Another hundred kilometers and the restricted region began, the area stretching almost to the West Coast where no one except agroplanners was allowed. The only thing high-intensity farming didn't need was people.

He heard the swoosh of a door and turned to see Egi Tsu and Ann Shita come in. The elder statesman was in his Population Care VIP uniform and the female assistant in her Hundred-Forty mission outfit.

"I apologize for wanting to see you this late," Soong began.

"Nonsense," Egi smiled, coming toward him.

Soong greeted Egi formally. Old people liked to feel important. Soong thought that for a hundred and twenty-two-year-old, Egi looked surprisingly handsome with his white crewcut and truculent face of an ancient tortoise. To grant a Unisave member a late-night interview like this visibly flattered the former ZG president.

"I'm happy to meet you," Soong smiled.

"I thought we already did—at Rani Mazure's funeral."

"I'm afraid that was just a little before my time."

"She was a great lady. She once told me you can only talk about civilization when people feel they have more duties than rights in relation to society."

"I remember video of the funeral."

Egi sized him up with a mischievous smile. "So young, Dr. Ast."

"The twin cylinder thinks the colonies should be represented by a young person."

"Yeah, seniors have never sat on Unisave, although Rani and I . . ." Egi interrupted himself with a smile. "Some of us kind of resent that."

Soong found Egi's century-old accent both comical and forceful in its own way. He almost wanted to say that, to put it crudely, population care could not be said to be an old man's problem, that it was only natural if the Unisave seven were young. Instead, he said it had already been two years since he had replaced Ken Wei.

"Still on inhibitors?"

"No."

Egi's bushy white eyebrows shot up in a mute but eloquent question mark.

"Our profession is exempted in the colonies," Soong smiled. "Seems nobody wants virgin gynecologists."

"Sensible."

Ann Shita led them toward a pair of deep, comfortable chairs while they told each other it was indeed remarkable that they had not met before. Egi had followed Rani Mazure as Zero Growth president but he had no official title now although he spent his seemingly inexhaustible energies on fertility troubleshooting.

Shita asked if they wanted anything and Egi ordered chamomile tea. In deference to his host, Soong said he would also have a glass of tea. The matronly Shita buzzed and relayed the order to the secretary.

While they waited, they chatted about the Bo Lim appointment and the charm of living in Manhattan. It occurred to Soong that Shita had no intention of leaving them. He was disconcerted for a moment—he had expected a private interview—but since only he knew the significance of Egi's answers, he leaned back in the deep foam and made a compliment on the handsome library.

"All about fertility," Egi smiled with an expansive gesture toward the memory reels and the books.

"Impressive," Soong acknowledged.

But the conversation turned to innovations in architecture. Egi mentioned experiments with air pressure spraying of plastics that allowed people to make their own free-form living space. It wasn't terribly new of course; for ages architects had tried to involve people in modifying their cubbyholes, but these quick-drying plastics allowed for totally new dimensions.

"Some people turn their apartments into caves," Ann Shita cued in.

Soong nodded. He felt he had to get to the point but let Shita give other examples of popular efforts to individualize beehive living. As she talked, he reflected that the reason China and Japan of yore had never achieved close relations was perhaps that each thought of itself as the middle kingdom. When nations had disappeared, Tokyo had sought partners and, after

merging with the Sydney economy, formed the
Hundred Forty ecosystem, so-called for its position along the 140° longtitude even if Auckland
was actually thirty degrees east of the Tokyo-
Sydney axis. All racial differences hadn't been
homozenized out. You still saw tall broad-
shouldered girls with very dark blue eyes like
Shita among people from the Hundred-Forty
system. The ethnic traces that persisted were
supposed to explain why Southerners were solid
and optimistic and Northerners in the system
had a penchant for discipline, pessimism and
insecurity. Australians of yore had expected to
prosper; Japanese had regarded good fortune as
highly unnatural.

"But you wanted to see me, Ast," Egi asked as
if he had read his visitor's impatient mind.

Shita stopped talking.

"One can never know too much," Soong began. He needed some sort of intro and said it was
indeed a happy coincidence that his host and he
had obstetrics in common. "I wondered if I
could have your valuable opinion on some new
experiments in fertility control that, perhaps,
might alter certain statistics." He looked at Ann
Shita to see if the prospect of overhearing two
former gynecologists talk shop might chase her
out of the room but she only blushed and seemed
relieved when the tea arrived.

Egi took his chamomile sweetened. Shita
busied herself with sweetener, spoons and napkins.

Soong continued. "I was home during the recess, as you may know . . ."

"Consultations?" Egi asked and leaned forward as if he expected to be told some colonist state secret.

Soong answered correctly. "We're fourth power people."

"Of course, but municipal governments still replace some of you."

"All our decisions are metadetermined," he said patiently. "Closed ecology has very little forgiveness for goofs."

"But metadetermination is consulting in the widest sense, isn't it?"

"Out there, solutions tend to suggest themselves." It occurred to him that Egi was old enough to have seen the dawn of space industrialization.

"So you were home during your recess . . ." Egi waved him on with an impatient gesture.

Soong took his time. High-intensity farming of the kind they practiced in the colonies was, to put it mildly, an exact science, and, he continued, there was indeed little forgiveness for mistakes. Yields were always optimal and totally calculable. Seasons and weather didn't apply; temperatures, sunlight and humidity were constant and weeds, insects, rodents and disease didn't exist. From the first Barnal spheres of a century ago—a century ago when people in retarded ecosystems on earth were still producing more offspring than megacalories to feed them—the coefficient of food to colonists had been down to decimals. In the beginning, it had taken eighty hectares to feed the twenty-thousand colonists in a Barnal sphere. Improved solar mirrors, hydroponics and Eden industries with optimum concentrations of carbon dioxide as well as optimum conditions of light, temperature, humidity and nutrients had cut the space farm nourishing twenty-thousand to twenty-two hectars. Modern colonies housed twenty million each, but it had not been necessary to multiply biomass manufacturing by a thousand. Plants grew in styrofoam boards so nutrient solutions could be sprayed directly on the roots and, as on the planet, nitrogen fixation gave the food crops the ability to convert nitrogen from the air directly. Yields were now a hundred and sixty grams per square foot and all people needed was five kilos of food, water and oxygen per day. If he, as the colonists' Unisave member, had sounded the alarm seven weeks ago it was because agroplanners in the colonies always dealt in closed-circuit ecology and were therefore quite naturally the first to see the flashing warning lights.

"Lag-behind egosystems reached population stability in the twenty-first century," Egi interrupted.

"And a generation ago, total resources became finite."

"What you mean is that there is a mathematical possibility of earthside shortage."

"Longevity is still on the increase." It was awkward to talk geriatrics with a guy who was a hundred and twenty-two. "We're in a demographic imbalance again, with death rates falling faster than the stabilized, Unisave-imposed birth rates. We are, in effect, adding a whole new generation of living people every thirty years."

"Longevity is a social achievement, not a failure."

"At a sizable cost."

Egi leaned forward and said the old were becoming both older and younger, in a sense, that second careers kept seniors more productive for longer, that the whole problem needed rethinking. There were scientists who held that the using-up of resources always generated an increase in human inventiveness that made total resources in effect unlimited.

"Look what you've invented in the colonies." Egi smiled. "Haven't you shown that substituting new resources for old is perfectly feasible?"

"Only at considerable cost and a high chance of blunder," Soong said patiently. "The risk of catastrophe is always very real in space."

But Egi ignored him. The new generation of centenarians, he said, presented new opportunities. For the first time, most people knew their great-grandparents and their great-great-grandparents into adulthood. With the gift of time and good health, centenarians had more of a chance to learn new skills, to take up new interests. Life—or an important part of it—began after one hundred. "More people living longer does of course add to the overall picture, but from there to project famine in ten, twelve years . . ."

"That's what agroplanners are for."

"And that's what I say, *theoretical* shortages." Egi swallowed a noisy gulp of tea. "That's assuming nothing new will be discovered in the meantime. It reminds me of life expectancy. When I was born my life expectancy was eighty. But during my lifetime, computer intelligence was brought to bear on medical science and I'm now a hundred and twenty-two."

"And still going strong."

"And still going strong, thank you."

"In fact, one might say there's no way telling how long you may live."

Egi smiled, then his face froze as he realized what the colonist was saying.

"Our specialty is fertility, conception, the making of life," Soong said calmly. "Perhaps you and I tend to overlook the true breakthrough in the other end of the spectrum—the perpetuation of life."

"You mean . . .?" But Egi didn't finish his sentence.

"Of course that, too, is projection." Soong meant to be a little sarcastic, but Egi seemed plunged in dark bafflement. Instead Soong explained. For a long time now, UICs had been formulating hypotheses and planned critical experiments that humans on their own could never hope to achieve. For decades the UICs had helped formulate new theories to explain their own experimental findings. In biology, ultraintelligent computers had more than doubled life expectancy. "And they are still beavering away, aren't they? While we are sitting here, the dysfunctions that may lead to your death at a hundred and fifty are no doubt being worked on and by the time you're a hundred and fifty, those that may cause your terminal illness at two hundred will be solved.

"Ad infinitum."

"That's perhaps a bit much, but theoretically yes."

The elder statesman remained silent.

"More tea?" Shita asked.

Soong was there for a purpose and he leaned toward her and held out his glass. "The colonies,

climate control on earth, vastly increased food
production and an end of political squabbling
. . . the UICs have done a lot for us," he said
cheerfully as Shita poured. His purpose was certainly not to make Egi gloomy. "I'm looking forward to a long life myself."

Egi gave him a long sideways glance as Shita
filled his glass also.

"While I was home during recess," Soong continued, "I met with a number of researchers from
my native torus . . ."

Egi interrupted. "What I and a lot of other
people object to is that you won't be playing
gericide bingo yourselves," he said with a scowl.

"But the colonies were never overpopulated."
It was not the first time Soong had encountered
this kind of hostility during these past weeks. He
drank a sip of tea. The notion was unworthy of a
great man like Egi, he thought. It was like the old
argument at the dawn of the space age that as
long as there was disease, war and poverty,
earthside humanity shouldn't tax itself with the
moon and colonist expansion. When had
nation-states of the past waited for each other?
When had more advanced nations shared their
affluence with less progressive tribes. Indeed,
when had any system deliberately made steps
backwards to fall in line with the less fortunate?

But when Soong looked at his host again, he
saw a malicious smile on Egi's face.

"The colonies *will* be overpopulated, won't
they, if we're all going to live forever?" Egi's
red-brown eyes twinkled above the puffy bags.
"I mean the UIC's are busily whirring away for
you, too."

Shita allowed herself to smile a little.

It was too humiliating for Soong to admit he had never thought of that. "Theoretically, we will also be affected."

"Isn't that intolerable in a closed-circuit ecology?"

"We've always been in perfect balance of course."

"Of course, but you're looking forward to a long life."

Soong felt uncomfortable.

"That's what I mean," said Egi reading his thoughts. "You should be playing bingo yourselves, shouldn't you?"

Now it was Soong's time to smile. "Not necessarily. We can always build more colonies, whereas earth is finite."

Five minutes later, Soong had the conversation back on track. Egi had scored his point and relented gracefully. To Soong's hint that he was here to consult him, the elder scientist said he was perhaps not as informed as he would like to be. Researchers on his home colony, Soong began, had come up with something similar to the inhibitor additives that such beehives as Algiers and Djakarta had tried. The Population Control people on his torus had tested a menses-inducing estriol derivative that could be added to municipal water supplies.

Egi nodded gravely.

Yes, the implications were momentous, Soong continued. Estriol fluoridation would free women from capsulating and free Population Care boards from the task of keeping tabs on everybody. The bioethic benefits were incalculable. People would no longer feel under the constant scrutiny of Population Care, quotas and non-quota penalties could be abolished since no one could cheat.

"But how do you allow for *some* conceptions?" Egi asked.

"Precisely," he smiled. He could see Shita was uncomfortable. "Estriol fluoridation is too perfect."

His ploy was working, he felt, as he let Egi ponder the dilemma and its social engineering solution. He could almost see Tsu's mind lock in on the problem and grope, logically, toward the way out—to cease fluoridation for so-and-so many days or weeks, probably on a rotating basis, of various sectors of an ecosystem so as to allow a predetermined number of random conceptions to occur.

"And there are no adverse effects?" Egi asked.

"We are still testing, but none so far."

"Then it could probably be refined to correspond to rigorous zero growth," Egi said, finishing his tea. Again, if there are no adverse effects, I guess your estriol fluoridation is acceptable."

Soong nodded gravely as if grateful for Egi's well-reasoned approach and said test studies were being conducted on one million women in eighteen colonies. As Shita served a third cup of tea, Soong sought the answer he had come for. "Would you say that with such a program we could reach . . . a point where we would actually have a negative birth rate earthside?" he asked, trying to sound casual.

"We already have, I'm sure," Egi smiled.

For Soong, the rest of the meeting was anticlimactic. His worst fears had been confirmed. His palms were sweaty but his voice was even when he asked—and Egi confirmed, that they were probably talking about nothing more than decimal points of below-zero in planetary birth-rates. He promised he would give Egi the first available data on the estriol tests and pretended to be interested when the conversation drifted toward the new Unisave session and the difficulty of finding decent apartments in Manhattan. Shita had just been through the ordeal.

"I can imagine," Soong said, getting up.

At the exit, he thanked both of them and reiterated his promise to forward data on the colonist research as soon as it became available.

The mission car took him back to Manhattan in twenty minutes. When the acceleration pressed him gently against the backseat, he told himself not to do anything rash. Negative growth could mean so many things, could upset so many graphs. The ground car changed in the riddle of holes that were the mouths of new tunnels. People who died before they procreated were negative growth, so were bachelors and spinsters and people who remained childless and refused to sell their quotas. He had lied to Tsu Egi but he had obtained his answer. To lie was antisynergetic and against all bioethics, but he needed to know. He could still hear himself ask whether estriol fluoridation might bring negative growth. "We're already there, I'm sure," Egi had said. Decimal points, no doubt, but how could the colonies have missed it? Or was Egi's remark a hunch, something demographers kept in the back of their minds, something that was theoretically possible? Had Egi said it in spite? He realized he had never met an old scientist who was as sharp as Egi, that in fact the oldest one he knew was his now former colleague Misha Sev.

Decimal drops in birthrates didn't mean gericide was no longer necessary earthside since the mushroom was growing, but it blunted the urgency. It invited evasion and delay. He leaned forward against deceleration as the car crawled up from the Holland Tunnel and melted into the West Side tracks. As he had told Egi, agroplanning was an exact science. So many hectars vs. so many people, so many megacalories to be metabolized by so many stomachs. Unido knew exactly how many megacalories the climate-controlled earth could produce. Because of the mushroom, Unido's flat-out production line would be bisected by Unisave's ascending population curve. It was as simple as that.

He told the driver to pick him up at 0915 and hurried past the scanners into his building. On the way up the gravity elevator, he told himself to be cautious in interpreting earthside people. He remembered his mother's warning before his first orientation year here. A lot of what people did on the planet was unintelligible, she had told him, because earthlings had little perspective. They were so close to their problems they couldn't see them half the time. And there was still a lot of planetary chauvinism.

He entered his apartment and saw the time was 0110. In some ten hours the session would begin. He had learned a lot during his two years on the planet, even if there were still things that astonished him. Despite homogenization, New Yorkers were past-oriented in quaint areas. They

often chose their mates because of looks instead
of intelligence, they never called things normal
but special. Everything was special. They loved
piped-in music everywhere and when they
wanted to pay someone an outrageous compliment they said he was artistic. But some of them
were intuitive and terribly clever. Like Zeke
Dua's wife, Tina. At the Duas' weekend for Unisave members and personnel last summer, he
had watched how she was attentive to everyone,
how she was smiling, soothing and graceful.
Mocking, too—referring to the colonies as
"happy valleys." He had played tennis with Nilo
Dor and pingpong with Misha Sev. He had gone
swimming with Tok, his wife and their little son
and daughter and, with one of Zeke Dua's assistants, explored the premordial lighthouse. Before the city had expanded out on the continental shelf, Montauk had been on the tip of Long
Island; now it was a government landmark. Dua
had the Hoo administration's permission to en-
tertain colleagues and the summer weekends at
Montauk had become something of a Unisave
tradition.

Last summer was the first time he had felt at
ease among people from different ecosystems.
General Belem had told about his experiences in
Brazil's Hundred Year Civil War. Iyabo had been
there with her sick husband, who had said that,
microbiologically speaking, life was a series of
improbable states. One evening Tina asked the
men to build a fire in the giant fireplace. He had
never seen anything so premordial and, together
with Zad, had sat and watched the flames. Even
after Zad had gone to her room, he had stayed
and watched the fire die. Another night Tina had

organized a game where all gave her a personal
item and she drew an article at random from
under a napkin and the owner told its story. He
had given his digital but there had been no fas-
cinating story, certainly nothing like Sal's wallet
floating on the Amazon for two days, or Iyabo's
zigzag ring that her great-grandmother had worn
at her wedding in Lagos. He had just sat and
watched Tina, especially. She was so graceful,
so knowing. It was unfair to compare Zad Gran
with Tina because Mrs. Dua was so much older
and sophisticated. Zad was his own age and a
second generation colonist. She was the best of
his mission assistants, but interpreting feminine
motives was sometimes more difficult than as-
sessing the impulses of people from various
ecosystems. Even Nagpur had astonished him.
The night he had told the chairman about his
upcoming proposal, Nagpur had asked whether
the colonies intended to cut off the powersats if
earth didn't agree to geriatric sanitation. The
idea was planetary and premordial and had
never occurred to him or anyone in the colonist
council. It was not the way space dwellers would
think. Once you had spent time in space, even on
a lowly powersat, and started at earth from fifty
thousand kilometers away for a year or so, your
conscience stabilized and you lost the competi-
tiveness and territoriality that was behind so
much of old earthside aggression. He thought of
his mother. Before his last return here, she had
made him promise he wouldn't feel guilty.

He was glad he was a colonist, not because
gericide didn't concern the colonies—or his
mother—but because space gave you a different
sense of direction, a different sense of reality. It

gave you dignity, too, and demanded fraternity
in return. A human being could not exist alone
in space. When he was home, he felt he was part
of the answer. Down here he sometimes had the
sense of living the end of an era. Maybe that was
what his mother meant. Whether you belonged
to one era or to the other was not a matter of guilt
or morality. Some people he had met here shared
this sentiment of living guilt-free. There were
places here where the pebble was dropped and
there were outlying areas that had been passed
by. People in left-behind regions were insecure
and hostile when they were made aware of how
far they were from the center of progress. But
that was silly; civilization was no longer geocentric.

5

Sal Belem pushed Viv Bord, Dal Far and the
others ahead of him toward the elevator with
smiles all around, renewed assurances and, for
Dal and the other men, backslaps. Nilo Dor
stayed behind.

"It would be good to be as efficient as the
Amcans are without having to be like them," Viv
smiled, laying her bejeweled hand on his arm as
he pressed for the elevator.

"You certainly are," he said.

"My maternal grandfather is Philadelphian."
Viv's gray-amethyst eyes looked up in his for a
fleeting second.

A stream of bilingual goodnights punctuated the massing into the gravitic elevator. The Queen Bee was the last to say goodnight, reaching up to peck Sal's chin. "And give Fel my love," she trilled.

"She'll be here Firday."

"We must get together."

Sal let the doors close. He heard the departing guests' dialogue echo in the shaft as they rode down, with Dal's booming Interlingua drowning Viv's cooing neo-Portuguese and the others' accompanying laughter. The get-together had been quintessential Sal Belem—light and improvised. As he walked back into the apartment, he decided such midnight receptions were not without benefits.

Nilo Dor was also ready to leave.

"Have another cognac," Sal told his senior adviser while he let himself fall down on the long sofa. He was too keyed up to go to bed right away. "Isn't she something?"

"Miss Bord knows everybody."

"Still . . . to find out the brother-in-law is on a research torus." Sal pursed his lips in appreciation.

"On the Cyclops project." Nilo remained noncommittal.

"Radio astronomer. I still don't see the connection though."

"Nor do I." Nilo poured himself a finger of the precious twenty-first century Hennessy in a clean brandy glass. "Maybe there isn't any."

"You know, I trust Viv's reactions. Sometimes they're violent but they're always positive."

"Eti Par thinks Lim is the tough replacement and Dal says someone in the Moscom mission who knows Lim calls him a smart guy."

"But why a 'tough' replacement?"

The Caracan shrugged. "Makes them *look* smart."

Sal liked his deputee's studied aloofness.

"To be tougher than Misha will be difficult," Sal yawned. There had been women like Misha in the army, totally different from the society ladies like Viv Bord. Every mission had a Viv, it seemed. Wasn't Tina Dua the Amcans' Viv? If the Duas' soirees and weekends were so popular it was because Zeke's wife was a stimulating woman of unerring taste, even if she was less flamboyant and quirky than Viv. People sought out Tina Dua for her confidence and wit.

"My hunch is that it has to do with age," Sal said.

"You'll find out tomorrow."

"It has to do with age because they're sure gericide will happen."

"What's our concensus?"

Sal hesitated. "We're a little different. The war made us less top-heavy." It was true, the South-cone had the smallest geriatric mushroom. "And still, our polls favor sanitizing."

Nilo downed his brandy in one gulp. "When's your wife coming?"

"Friday." Sal got up.

"I have several invitations for her."

"Is the acclimatizer on? It stinks in here." Sal crossed to the curtain himself and saw the recycling was on maximum.

"Maybe we should get some sleep."

Nilo left five minutes later, softly closing the door. Sal Belem ran a tight ship—the smallest office of any of the Seven. His personal staff included a handful of New Yorkers, five Sao Pauleans, two Bogotans, Del Far and his staff and of course Nilo. He got along very well with the Caracan, probably because they both saw the world the same way, in black and white. He knew there were drawbacks to such a view, but there were also advantages.

He undressed, flipping his uniform on the sofa, and went to bed thinking about Misha and about her replacement, whose brother-in-law was a radio astronomer in a Jovian orbit. Every other person had a relative in space. Not quite every other person, but an awful lot of people lived in tin can habitats out there and a lot more of the best young men and women were recruited every year. All of them looked back on earth as Old World pioneers looked back on Europe for a couple of centuries.

He turned on the wallscreen and saw a detachment of U.S. Cavalry ride across the wall. A lot of left-behinds resented the idea of finding the future staked out in advance by the elite in the colonies. But so it was, and colonists even made fun of this resentment. "You must stop thinking geocentrically," Soong Ast had chided once. "The move out was in response to the crisis of insufficient energy and food and room to live."

But the colonists weren't saddled with a geriatric mushroom. On the wall, the cavalry chased Indians left to right. A premordial film. He watched his bedside digit and saw it was 0233. He was wide awake and the cavalry kept coming, now surrounding an Indian tent village. Again the colonies had sensed tomorrow's mood. He hadn't told Nilo, but the figures he saw this morning before leaving Buenos Aires heavily favored some sort of sanitation.

The war had sanitized the Southcone of a lot of over-sixty citizens. Once the hemisphere had been full of them—powerful and vicious old men. Poor men were different; they faded into the jungle when they heard soldiers coming. He had had four hundred men with him the day they razed Monteiro. They had landed a hundred kilometers upstream and seen the villagers flee into the unconditioned rain forest. Only two women stayed in front of the stilt houses as if the hundred-year war had nothing to do with them. He and his men burned down the village but allowed the two women to toss their belongings into plastic washbasins. One of the women said the guerrillas were an hour's march upstream and Fons stayed behind with sixty men and the landing hover. The trail winding along the river was narrow and probably booby-trapped. After twenty minutes they surprised a column of old people coming down the trail. Almost all the seniors disappeared into the jungle but a couple of them stopped when ordered to. He had them frisked and fall in behind the women at the head of the column. The trail ended in a clearing. After a while he spotted a small footbridge and ordered the column to form again. The first woman hesitated, but crossed. The second woman followed, but as she neared the other side the first woman stepped to the right to leave passage. First the washbasin rolled down the embankment, then her body, flung into the air by the explosion. The seniors had never said a word.

On the wall, a prehomogenized white woman

huddled behind a tent clutching an Indian child as the cavalry completed the encirclement. He was sure colonist bingo would be played differently among the powerful. If you were the top dog you imposed your own rule. Before homogenization, the hemisphere's most passionate problem had always been the nature of a dictator and the mechanisms that sustained dictatorships.

He missed the years in the unconditioned jungle. Or sometimes he did. After station identification, the cavalrymen set fire to the tents and chased more frightened Indian women and children. The white woman, it turned out, was the fiancee of the youngest of the cavalry officers. That night back in Monteiro he had told his recorder, "one dead." One unidentified female. He had attributed the casualty to the rebels. It was their landmine.

A century ago ultraintelligent computers had made classical nuclear warfare impossible. The UICs of the old United States and the Soviet Union had communicated with each other with enormous speed and effectively fused their identities. People were so much slower, talking to each other at the snail's pace of a hundred and fifty words a minute, and until homogenization they had remained apart, antagonistic and tribal. The civil war hadn't been fought with UICs and had dragged on and on. In hindsight at least that was obvious.

At the next commercial, he saw it was 0259. He turned off the video, but the sudden silence made him wide awake. Oneness had come with the colonies—from a few thousand kilometers out the one-planet-one-people idea became self-evident—but the end of the war had come like all other ends, when people had had enough. He got out of bed and crossed to the acclimatizer. Air was vital. He pushed it to maximum again. He had never understood how people could sleep in recycled air; work, yes, but sleep no. Recycled air was like air in old churches, like the air in Alegre the second after he had given the order to fire. The stillness for a split second. Then the screams started, people falling, other running, some trying to mass into the federal building. The whole thing had lasted less than seven minutes; he had looked at his digit when he ordered the fire in front of the governor's palace and when they were at the bottom of the steps, one solid mass of khaki. In seven minutes, resistance in the North had been broken.

He might be rotting in some peacetime garrison in Buenos Aires or up North if it hadn't been for Alegre. The dice had rolled for him on top of the steps that afternoon. Peace had been wonderful and the hemisphere had fused its identity. He had married Fel the day after his promotion. They had spent their honeymoon in Mexico City, visiting the Pyramids and spaceports. A year later, he had been back in Mexico City as head of the ecosystem delegation to the ZG conference and learned how war had isolated *Cono sur*, the hemisphere's new official name.

He hadn't thought of Alegre for years. The mob had jeered and taunted his soldiers for days, and for days he had ordered them not to react. He could still see the faces when the photon guns started to sear, the expressions of stupid disbe-

lief as people shriveled and fell. The surprise
had been total. At the military academy they
never taught him that wars and revolutions were
won and lost in moments when the totally unexpected happened, but he had waited for such a
moment. After Alegre, Curatiba capitulated
without a shot and two weeks later the Sixteen
Points were accepted by both sides.

His surprise in Mexico had been to discover
world consensus. ZG was not against the grain of
popular opinion, as he had imagined when they
had appointed him titular head of the hemisphere delegation. He had never been close to
scientists, but since he was head of the mission,
he had ordered each one of them to report to him
every night and to tell him in plain Interlingua
what they had found significant in their day's
activities in metapanels and seminars. Late at
night in his hotelroom he had talked a report into
his recorder, just like during the war. Writing
had never been easy for him, so his reports were
short, essential and to the point.

The Sal Belem ZG Report had been in print a
month later and it had made him a household
word throughout the hemisphere. When the
General Assembly voted Unisave into existence,
Joa Guz of Caracas had been the obvious choice
to fill the system's seat. What finally defeated
Guz had been his five children. Latins were sensitive to ridicule and a father of five couldn't
represent the Southern Cone in a new fourth
power agency dedicated to absolute zero. Although he knew precious little about Population
Care, demographics, future planning or negative
growth, Brigadier-General Belem had suddenly

looked right. But that was seven years ago. Tomorrow, they would get down to the business of playing a real God committee.

6

Iyabo Att woke up as the room filled with a haunting tune. A throaty woman's voice sang of the pain of feeling your heartbeat. A stream of metallic light slid through the venetian blinds. Twentieth century jazz was night music, she thought. It was probably only in Manhattan that strange stations sent soulful cries of hurt and lost love soaring on the airwaves around the digit.

She got up and ran into the waterroom. . . *the joy that would last until the end of time,* the carbon voice swirled after her. She hopped into the shower wondering why she didn't have morning sickness.

By the time she had wrapped herself in a towel and walked back into the bedroom the station had switched to contemporary music, and when she got into her uniform it was playing a classic, Abba or Hubert Law. She called her office and told Trantor she was on her way. She was hungry. Maybe that was the sign, together with her sleeping like a rock. She cut the radio in midwail and called Tok. His morning face came on the screen and she cooed a good morning full of meaning.

"No matter what, let's have dinner tonight," he grinned.

"No matter *what*?"

"No matter whether there will be an emergency reception for our new boy or what."

She suddenly loved him, madly and irresponsibly. He told her what Bo Lim had said at the skyport. He told her Zeke's idea that Misha's age was an embarrassment to Moscom in this wondrous world of youth but her eyes stopped him.

"How old are you Tok?" she asked.

"A tantalizing thirty-seven."

"You're much too young for me."

"New boy Bo is thirty-three, if you want a kid your own age."

"I feel reckless this morning."

"You look it."

Their minds fluttered around each other like butterflies while he told her about the Bo Lim skyport interview he had just seen on the 0800 news. Jammu himself had tooled out to the skyport at dawn to greet the new man.

"I imagine so much about you," she interrupted.

"It's the same for me," he answered.

"Meanings flow so unhindered now." What she meant was that they were no longer crippled by the need to defy and justify; not to each other at least. "Now, I can see right through you."

"And what do you see?"

"Things that matter."

"Nothing else?"

"Vanity fishing for compliments," she winked.

They looked at each other on the screen and she thought of her husband, of how much Tunde had taken from her in the end. Tok and she were also a way of healing, a way of putting the past behind her. Their love was not only sweet, unsuspected cravings and mutual regards, but a curious new gravity.

"Tonight, no matter what," she said.

"And in the meantime?"

"Reading your thoughts across the horseshoe."

"Have a feeling it'll be a short meeting today, getting Lim settled in and recapping where we are."

He kept talking and she felt it didn't matter what they said, that below the words were feelings and secret tensions. Love was to give and to be given to. And it was looking forward and anticipating.

She looked at him.

"How do you feel?" he asked tenderly.

"We're fine."

He answered her with one of his sheepish little-boy smiles. "See you up there," he winked.

She whispered a "bastard darling" as they hung up.

Impulsively, she decided to change. She hadn't appeared in a traditional dress since . . . since when in fact? She wanted to look regal. She zipped down her uniform, stepped out of it and walked into the bedroom. The gossip stations would love it. Iyabo Att caused a diplomatic ripple today entering in the flowing robes of UNCTAD womanhood. If her hair had been long she would have plaited it. Where was Olu now? As schoolgirls they had plaited each other's hair. Olu had been a fiery little creature who always needed to be helped and had married an intense young man from Lagos with sad eyes and long delicate hands.

She slipped into a dress and began to tie the lengths of bands around her waist. Universities had fawned over her after the Nobel prize and she had lectured in robes a few times. She hadn't worn a robe since Rani Mazure's funeral. Or was it at the ceremony in Stockholm when the Academy president had called Tunde and her UNCTAD's Marie and Pierre Curie. Robes would have made her look too healthy next to Tunde.

It had been his last happy year. They had traveled. Tunde had been offered professorships in a dozen cities where they visited to seek second opinions. She had wondered later if it was then that he first knew he was incurable. She had stayed in Manhattan for the Unisave session and Tunde had returned to the Pasteur Institute.

Funny that she should be in love with a Parisian now. Between treatments and her weekend visits, Tunde had continued to work with Mor and Sil on the cell theory. He had never allowed her to feel particularly martyred, even at the end when he was confined to the wheelchair and he could do little more than sit and think, memorizing long strings of equations and dictating the results to Mor. She added four more pins in the back of the headscarf and scrutinized the total effect in her mirror.

When she arrived at her office she was greeted with doubletakes that melted into approving smiles. While Dosh made fiber toasts and coffee, Trantor asked what was the occasion.

"No reason," she lied, sitting down with care. Dresses weren't made for slim office furniture.

"Women like to astonish, you know."

Dosh said she was herself too big for robes as she corrected several folds in the back of the headscarf. Trantor read the messages—invitations to UN receptions, including one for plenipotentiaries and head of mission people only, two missives from Nairobi, one from Bayo extending the municipal government's wishes for a fruitful session, the other from Oti requesting two video interviews. "And Fagbure called to confirm the dinner tonight."

She had forgotten. Gab Fagbure was a big man, both in girth and in UNCTAD affairs and she *had* promised. Maybe she could bring Tok. It could be done casually, she arriving on the arm of her colleague.

"Tell you what," she told Trantor. "Call up Tok Sort—both at his office and his apartment—and leave a message saying I'm extending an invitation to him to attend Fagbure's dinner party with me tonight."

Trantor went into the front office to call the Eurocom mission.

Gab and Kofu. He was a former video editor and she the head of the Central UNCTAD Council. Gab's attributes and functions were as many as they were murky—so many things in UNCTAD politics were subterranean. Kofu was famous because she had once produced a risque play on Afrovision and had spent a ridiculous week in confinement. She was funny.

"Tok Sort says he will be delighted," Trantor called from the door. "Do you want me to confirm to the Fagbures?"

"Please do, yes." She was happy. Tok understood that Fagbure's party was something she

had forgotten, something she couldn't get out of.
One of the delights of being in love—reasonably
in love—was to understand things half said. If
love was this sweet complicity, she was in love.
If it meant elaborate games and losing one's bearing, she was not in love. She had never understood all-consuming passion. Few people did
nowadays. Maybe Tok's acceptance just meant
he was a civilized lover—naughtily, she savored
the premordial word—who understood a lady's
predicament. Yet that wasn't him either. If she
was attracted to anything beyond his agile self-
assurance and charmpot irresistibility, which he
knew so well how to use, it was his ruffled
frankness. His bioethics. She was sure he could
talk himself in and out of everything, but also
that he would never live a mesh of ambiguity
and escalating lies.

Their position was vulnerable—and escalating. They were members of an institution which
reached into the deepest recesses of every human. In certain regions they were better known
than ecosystem leaders. What human resources
class didn't study Misha's *Population Cycles*?
What twelve-year-old didn't know Jammu was
the modern Bengali abbreviation of Jammian-
wakky?

It was typical of Tok to have skipped restric-
tion. Besides, as he had told her last night, Kikki
had been restricted after the birth of their daughter, meaning that so long as he was faithful to her
his snubbing the law was nothing more than a
little private joke.

One of them would have to resign, or both of
them, if she went through with it and named him
the father. She told herself that, today at least,

she didn't mind. They could be replaced. Look at
Misha and, two years ago, Ken Wei. Of course
she could also not go through with it and instead
they could regularize their situation. Tok could
have himself restricted, get a divorce, then petition his Population Care board to be derestricted.
Derestriction had been one of the thorniest
amendments to their basic law and it had come
about as a logical extension of the absolute right
of everyone to replace himself but only himself.
It rarely happened of course, but if an open-
quota girl married a closed-quota divorcee, her
right to replace herself was infringed upon if she
couldn't have her offspring with whomever she
chose. They had never solved the issue satisfac-
torily but allowed such mismatched couples to
petition for derestriction of the closed-quota
partner although it made an infinitesimal
number of people fathers or mothers of one-
point-five children.

With Misha's replacement she was now the
only woman on Unisave. That, too, made it more
difficult—Unisave's only lady knocked up and
giving birth to a quota by father unknown. Yet,
she wanted it, deeply. The child would also be a
homage to Tunde, to his crippled being and to
the invicibility of his mind. She could see him,
puckish and myopic, in his chair pecking at his
terminal and saying the messy details of existence were nothing compared to the jokes of
molecular life. Amyotropic lateral sclerosis, or
ALS as Tunde called the disease that wasted the
voluntary nerves and muscles, didn't escape the
UICs but Tunde's case was too advanced. In the
end, when Tunde's speech had been so badly
affected that only those who knew him well

could understand what he was saying, his office was filled with gadgets like pageturners and his terminal equipped with special controls and he and Mor were applying biological probabilities to sociology. Why did social engineers reject them out of hand? If anything, they should be the first to realize that patterns of life were the frontier of knowledge.

Mor had been in Manhattan two months ago and she owed him and Fran a call. They had been more helpful than most when Tunde died, arranging many vexing details that she had only discovered much later.

She still had weeks to decide and in the meantime she could daydream of a time when having a child was always bioethical and legal. Eight years ago there had been no Unisave. Of course people had been less equal, which was why, despite Tok's sarcasm, she had voted with Soong Ast six weeks ago. The colonist had been eloquent that day. Geriatric bingo was the only just way to absolute zero, he had said, because if all men are equal, two men must be worth the double of one. To save two by eliminating a third is just. She had resented Tok's poking, his gibes about the *will* to live, his half-serious suggestion that they stack the odds against hundred-and-twenty-year-olds and the chronically ill, his wondering whether one pound of sixty-year-old flesh wasn't worth more than one pound of ninety-year-old flesh. She had voted for Soong because the colonist's proposal said all men were equal, period, and she felt Sal Belem had voted with Soong and her for the same reason. The general's heart wasn't bleeding for geriatric Latinos—Sal's heart probably couldn't bleed at all—but he couldn't vote otherwise. War had made the Brazilian hard and indifferent, but it had also made him incorruptible.

Trantor buzzed to say Fagbure was on two. She turned toward the desk visor as Gab's big face came on. His first words were a compliment. "Robes suit no one as beautifully as you, my darling," he smiled.

"Flattery will get you nowhere," she laughed back.

"So we will see you both tonight?"

"I knew you wouldn't mind."

"Two Unisave members at my party; everybody will be green with envy."

She thought she caught a glimpse of something in Gab's truculent eyes.

"About 2000?"

"Or even later, if you prefer."

When his face faded from the screen she still wondered what to make of the glint in Gab's eyes.

7

"Well, she's tall and she's the girl everybody wants. She's breezy in a sort of magazine cover kind of way."

Tina Dua was on the phone and Zeke dug into a second fiber muffin.

"Yes, he's right here," she smiled. She looked across at him and asked loud enough for Aly Fem to hear whether it was a state secret that he was home. She listened to Aly for a moment then looked at him. "Poor Zeke darling, no. He had to spend the night at the White House and couldn't sleep. Positively spooky."

The audio conversation drifted back to the girl while Tina continued to pluck her eyebrows. Zeke barely listened. Tina was selling someone on the Fems again. How many plays were cast like this, not by lecherous closed-quota producers but by their wives' best friends over morning coffee. How would Tina sell *him*? Well, you see, Aly, Zeke has this kind of lived-in face that audiences love in a man. And the years on Unisave have made him a perfect ham, a natural actor! He poured himself a third cup. Covering the mouthpiece with one hand, Tina whispered that the play was about a marriage falling apart because two people never stop lying to each other.

"Open-quota girl seduced by married but unrestricted cad?"

But she was back with Aly. Tina never used the visiplate of a phone, never showed herself on any screen, in the morning. "She'd be absolutely marvelous, darling."

He had another twenty minutes and pulled out the synopsis of Bo Lim's book. Maybe it would be a short opening with everybody greeting the new man and adjourning until tomorrow. He hadn't slept much in the creaky West Wing. Hoo had called him at dawn for the working breakfast.

"I think George must be attracted to the younger woman," Tina purred. "It must be physical, too, if you see what I mean."

He looked at the resume of *Nitrogen Fixation*.

The Demographics Department aide who had
escorted him from the working breakfast knew
precious little about Bo Lim— a skeleton bio and
this resume, synopsized in eight neat pages.
Born in Minsk in 2155; married, two children.
That made Lim thirty-three, five years older than
Soong Ast. Very clever of Moscom. Members of
plenipotentiary committees were appointed by
their ecosystems, but once appointed they were
fourth power, responsible to the General Assembly alone. Very few appointees were replaced by
manipulating home systems since their success
was measured in constant metapolls, but the fact
that municipalities *could* replace a person gave
them the illusion of foreign policy as it had
existed before the whole-earth perspective.

"They are dying to print something naughty
about you, of course they are," Tina laughed,
making enormous eyes across to him.

He picked up the synopsis and read that there
was no area of recombinant DNA technology
that had paid handsomer dividends for humanity than nitrogen fixation. The opening sentence
made him wonder whether he was reading Bo
Lim or the Demographics Department synopsis
writer. Early gene splicing had led to triumphs
in antiobiotics and vitamins and had revolutionized immunology in less than seventy
years, but nitrogen fixation had increased
biomass tenfold by giving food crops the genetic
ability to convert nitrogen from the air directly
into chemicals for growth. In one sweep, nitrogen fixation had reduced planetary dependence
on expensive fertilizers.

Pretty turgid. He vaguely tuned in on Tina's
telephone conversation while he skimmed over

the next five pages. The text smelled of translation from Interlingua.

"Following the trends from head to toe is ridiculous."

He wondered.

"It's silly when a person misses the humor of fashion."

Did Moscom think the way around gericide was through bioengineering?

"She has a way of wearing every possible current trend all at once."

He realized Tin and Aly weren't talking about the actress anymore, but that didn't mean that Moscom bioengineers couldn't have made a breakthrough. Was Lim going to reveal some self-perpetuating Andromeda strain of protein that would make gericide superfluous? But wasn't that Unido's turf? The forum to reveal that a new recombinant DNA technique might be applied to agriculture was Unido, not Unisave. He didn't know much about the frontiers of bioengineering, but like everyone else he knew that progress in agroplanning was hard to come by. The search for edible biomass had driven Unido outward into increasingly hostile environments, capital outlays that were enormous and risks that were staggering. Biomass investments were eligible for "plowback" credits in all systems because Unido was knocking against the ceiling where it took five kilos of food, water and oxygen to create five kilos of food, water and oxygen.

Tina was back talking about the actress, saying the girl's success was her strong, stark, clean look. He dropped the synopsis, telling himself that there was of course no reason why there

should be a direct connection between Lim's
bioengineering past and his Unisave appointment. Iyabo, too, came from the life sciences.
Misha came from demographics.

"She projects a kind of innocence and power,"
Tina said, adding that the girl's career had been
wobbly, from modeling to acting, but that she
had learned from her mistakes. He watched Tina
as she agreed to a luncheon and said she would
haul him along to the opening. She looked
across at him to make him agree and with a few
more assurances hung up.

"Just impossible," she sighed dramatically.
"I'm sorry Zeke. Fresh coffee?"

Before he could answer she had poured him a
fourth cup. "You simply must promise to make
yourself free on the tenth. I told Aly we would
attend. What are you reading?"

"Potting tips . . . a summary of our new man's
book."

"Do you think he'd care to attend?"

"Bo Lim?"

"You can invite him. General Belem, too. It's
this kind of support we need."

"You'll have us all arrested on morals
charges," he smiled.

"Tok Sort, too, and . . ." She looked across at
him with a sudden dramatic squint. "What's he
been telling you?"

He raised his eyebrows.

"He's your friend," she said matter-of-factly.

"What do you mean?"

"Tell me, is Kikki in town?"

"No, I don't think so."

"So it is true."

He was totally lost. "What's true?"

"The most viciously naughty rumors that he's having an affair with some UNCTAD head of mission. Viv Bord told me."

"You're cra . . ." He stopped. Tina hated him when he was too bumblingly innocent. "You know, men rarely confide in each other about such things."

"You positively boast about such things!"

"Tok's as busy as the rest of us, before the session and everything."

But she scrutinized his eyes. In a low voice, she asked "You *did* spend the night at the White House?"

He held her gaze, wondering whether she was kidding, then decided to take her seriously. It was more flattering. "I showed you—on the visiphone."

She got up. "I'll call your office and have Lan keep your evening of the tenth open then," she said in her ordinary voice. She gave him another glance and said he looked awful. "Hope it'll be a short session today. You need rest, Zeke."

As he got his briefcase, she explained that reviving *Who's Afraid of Virginia Woolf* was a bold piece of showmanship. Fem was putting on an unabridged version, which meant not cutting the last act where Martha makes love to the younger professor practically within her George's earshot to spite and humiliate him. Courage in the arts was as important as courage in Population Care, she added with a significant glance.

Getting into the UN ground car downstairs, he decided he would do everything to be available on the tenth. He owed Tina that. She had come to Oregon with him. What she meant of course was

that no morals squad would close down the Fem
production if the first two rows were filled with
UN diplomats and heads of mission. She said it
was a typical twentieth century play, an emotional rollercoaster where you got screamed at.
He wondered whether a thirty-three-year-old
Muscovite, whose only published memory reel
dealt with biomass engineering, could be interested. He'd try. In fact, he would invite them
all, Soong, too, although Tina called him "pro-
vincial." Only Tok would appreciate being
screamed at in a theater—although a play about
adultery might be too close for comfort. He
didn't know what to think of Tina's newest item.
No dazzling lady came to mind in the UNCTAD
mission, but Tina's gossip usually was deadly
accurate, even if it came from the Southcone's
Viv Bord.

The car decelerated and surfaced on Forty-
Second and Lexington. The morning traffic was
still heavy and the chauffeur leaned over and
asked if he should turn on the siren.

"Not yet!" He hated all ostentatious blaring of
UN sirens and racing up First Avenue like some
potentate from a fifth-rank municipality. Belem
had done that a couple of times.

In the beginning, Zeke had found Sal a living
example of the Neanderthal past when armed
conflicts were thought of as solutions and mid-
dleclass sons believed they could become gentlemen aristocrats by way of military careers.
Wallenstein, Napoleon, Eisenhower and Poiret.
History was full of men who, like Belem, had
used the army to climb up from humble origins.
Lately, Zeke had come to like the big Brazilian.

Belem had an instinct for the visceral; he played no games, yet had a gift for seizing opportunities.

They swung up First Avenue. The driver turned on the siren, slid out of the gravity tracks and accelerated.

"You can turn it off now," Zeke winced. Four hundred meters from the entrance the driver flipped off the siren and they coasted smartly to the old UN gate.

In the office, Zeke was greeted by Lan and the rest of the staff. The five weeks' vacation had worked wonders, he thought. They were all brimming with enthusiasm.

"Anything I should know," he asked watching the wall digit. Lan, a tall thin girl with crisply curling hair, a square chin and a candid smile, said Tina had called to tell her not to accept any engagements on the evening of the tenth.

He went to his private waterroom for a minute and popped a quaracin. In the mirror, he did look tired. He hoped it would be a snappy meeting. Back in the front office, Bi Flan handed him his briefcase. Again, he asked if there was anything he should know before going into the meeting and again they all smiled disarmingly. He would pop in on Tok, he decided.

"Do you want me to call Bo Lim's office and arrange a private introduction?" Flan suggested.

"Too late now, but thank you." There was no special reason for meeting Lim at 1150, but it wasn't a bad idea. "I'll be in Tok's office if you need me," he said on the way out. He hesitated a second. Maybe Flan should call Lim and tell him about the informal ten-minute grace period. He thought better of it; he was sure Lim's own people would cue him in.

As he entered the Eurocom office, he was greeted by a gaggle of voices and the sharp glare of video lights. He was about to duck out again when Tok peered through the lights and waved him forward with an enthusiastic gesture.

"You all know Zeke Dua," Tok said in Interlingua and English. Several cameras swung around.

"I'll be right there," Tok laughed, deftly covering the nearest mike with a hand. Resuming in Interlingua, Tok continued his Mundovision interview. The reporters were young and aggressive, Zeke thought—or they were just jumping on the chance to get first-hand info on the planet's hottest story this morning. Tok talked about sexagenaria and said something about the problem being not how to define the possible but how to define the necessary. Switching to English for a second camera setup, Tok repeated himself. The problem was not what Unisave could do but what had to be done, he said, pointing to an off-camera digit to signify time was up.

One newsman swung around and focused his camerapen on Zeke.

"Also with us is Amcan's Dua," the reporter began in UNspeak. Before Zeke could escape, the newsman asked if the recess had altered anything in his ecosystem's view. A second camera and several sunguns were on him.

"Tok Sort just told us the tragedy is that we constantly juggle the possible and neglect the indispensible. Do you believe humankind is against the wall?"

"Do you believe our options are running out?"

"Metapolls are divided, sir."

Zeke answered that even at the risk of colliding with Unido's famine forecast, humankind obviously needed a humanistic approach. A third camera elbowed in on him and an accented voice asked if he questioned Unido's figures, or the colonists' interpretation of the figures.

Zeke felt trapped. "I'm merely saying we have ten years to look for solutions."

Someone behind a sungun asked if he was going to table a counterproposal.

"To avoid turning old age into a parody of life, we must give meaning to our younger years," he answered, wondering whether this was live or a taped interview he could turn his back on.

A female voice to his right asked him to elaborate. He turned slightly in her direction and stared into a camera eye that wasn't directly in the glare. "Life is priceless as long as it means something, and it means something as long as you can be compassionate about others, as long as you can love and, perhaps, hate." That was what he had told the students in Los Angeles two nights ago. "To give our own future old age dignity and meaning, we must have feelings now that will prevent us from looking back with regret."

The woman reporter asked if he thought Unisave should get into preparing people for old age.

"What I'm suggesting," he answered, "is that it's best to remain active as long as possible. Look at Sarah Akhmanova."

"Are you in favor of pushing back mandatory retirement?" the first reporter came back.

"Isn't the frontier between active and leisure living pretty blurred already?"

"Do you personally condemn joykillings?"

"Absolutely."

"But the mushroom keeps growing."

Suddenly Tok was next to him, smiling into the sunguns and cutting off the questions with bilingual pleas. The time was 1102. One by one the reporters turned the cameras on themselves and signed off with short, terse comments.

"I'm sorry I walked in on your news conference," Zeke told Tok.

"You're always good at setting the tone."

The reporters surrounded them. Tok shook hands and tapped shoulders all around and Zeke decided he couldn't decide whether his colleague was having an affair with some UNCTAD lady.

"Is Kikki in town?" he asked. It was none of his business but he wanted to be able to show Tina that he, too, could be *au courant*.

"She's in Paris, with the kids," Tok answered.

The woman reporter elbowed in on Zeke without her camera pack and asked him if he really believed gericide would *not* happen.

"Our decisions are metadetermined," he answered diplomatically.

She objected that there was no planetary concensus to make a symbiotic determination with.

Tok was lost in a cluster of other reporters.

"I know," Zeke smiled gravely.

"Will the final solution be UIC-imposed?" she asked with a hint of derision in her voice.

"That would be abdicating our judgment, wouldn't it?"

He could see she was thinking that so many

decisions had been abdicated to the prodigious calculators that long ago had outpaced the intelligence of their makers. But she simply looked at him and said old people had few defenders.

"Maybe because they're so many," he smiled gently.

She put a hand on his arm and a second later was lost in the crowd.

Zeke knew he looked lousy, but did he look so lousy the woman had felt a need to pat his arm in sympathy? Or was he overreacting again?

Jovially, Tok pushed the news crowd ahead of him.

"Let's go, Zeke," Tok grinned, stepping over powerpacks and cables and heading toward the door.

8

It was the assignment of the day. If only she could get there. Ter Ki pushed through the nineteenth floor security guards and newspeople, holding her ID high.

"Excuse me," she said as she pushed her way along the corridor. She was a little girl but she could see the entrance. "Excuse me." Microphones stood in clusters at several points and videoeyes fixed on long metallic fishpoles stood leaning against the walls. The hallway was humming with excitement.

Despite her uniform, she was challenged at the committee door.

"Ki?"

The smaller of the UN guards took her ID and pushed the card into the slit of his clipboard. When the ID scan ejected it with the familiar beep, the taller guard opened the heavy door and let her slip in. On the other side of the door was still another guard, but behind him she recognized chairman Nagpur himself.

She was there.

"Ki?" the guard asked in a hushed tone.

She nodded.

"Patel Nobu."

"Pleased to meet you," she whispered. The quiet of the committeeroom was almost scary after the noise in the hallway.

"You haven't worked this committee before," the guard murmured.

"No, I haven't." The room was like any other fourth power committeeroom but she couldn't help feel a tingling of awe and excitement. Quietly, she crossed to the secretary's desk below the chairman's podium at the open end of the delegates' horseshoe. The six swivel chairs stood neatly in their places around the three-quarter circle but there were no nameplates. How silly could she be? They had been sitting here for years.

She slipped into her seat below Jammu Nagpur, nodding up to him, but he didn't see her. At the door, guard Nobu smiled when she looked at his direction. Guards were funny; always so fatherly, even when they weren't any older than you.

She put down her handbag. She wanted to be ready when the others came in. At the door, Nobu crossed his arms on his chest and stood smartly with his legs apart. She sneaked another glance at the chairman. He was reading something.

She was nervous and began by checking the simultranslator. She had heard that the Unisave Seven all spoke English but maybe the new Muscovite . . . She leaned forward and whispered into the recessed mike, "Kto ne prokleenal stanstionik smotry-teley." Pushkin's short stories were as far as she had gotten in Russian. The simultranslator boomed back, WHO HAS NOT CURSED STATIONMASTERS . . .

"Excuse me," she blustered, cutting the volume.

The chairman leaned forward and looked down at her. She turned crimson.

"I don't think we will need that," he smiled.

Before she could think of an intelligent answer, he was back in his papers. At the door, Nobu grinned.

She checked the tape deck and the voting systems. She knew her line by heart. I hereby declare open the fourteen hundred and seventeenth meeting of the Plenipotentiary Committee for the Unified Salvation of the Human Race. Chairman Nagpur would begin and she would cue in with the minutes of the fourteen hundred and sixteenth session. "The prelipotentiary committee. . . .", etc. etc., "with the reduction of mankind the only topic on the agenda . . ." And so on. "La réduction de la race humaine," she whispered into the simultranslator and watched the needle as the monitor came back in barely audible Interlingua. She was ready. She had been watching a movie last night when Von Tin called with the assignment. Von hadn't said why, just, "Ter, you do Unisave tomorrow."

The door opened and Zeke Dua and Tok Sort came in. She thought they looked exactly as on video, the Amcan delegate ruffled and grown-up, and Sort suave and superior. God, it was exciting! She watched as Sort strode past her to Jammu Nagpur while Dua just smiled and nodded and sat down at what had to be his seat. Sort told the chairman that Dua had just defended the right to active aging on Mundovision. "Zeke here faced down the cameras and boomed, 'Life is priceless as long as it means something.' "

Dua smiled. "To understand anything you have to live a long time."

Dua's face seemed all vertical lines. She thought the Amcan delegate was handsome.

"A lady secretary today; the omens are favorable," Sort hummed with a slight bow in her direction. She felt her face flush and realized he noticed it.

"What's you name?" he asked.

"Ki. Ter Ki." She blushed even more. The stories were going around about Tok Sort. There were even rumors he was having an affair with UNCTAD's Iyabo Att. She didn't look up until she heard him talk to the chairman again.

It all happened too fast. They turned as the door opened and General Belem led a younger person ahead of him into the committeeroom. Outside, the guards pushed back the mediapeople and their videoeyes on long metal poles. Belem looked immense and Ter guessed the other man was the substitute Muscovite.

Belem was all smiles and confidence as he led the new delegate forward.

"Here we are, finally," the general grinned.

"Meet Bo Lim." Belem made the introductions. Dua stood up to shake hands in premordial fashion. Ter thought the Muscovite looked frightfully young in his brand-new delegate's uniform.

Turning to the chairman, Dua asked that they keep the meeting short today since Bo Lim had traveled all night.

"Don't prevail on me," Jammu said above her. "Prevail on yourselves and check your eloquence."

Lim smiled politely as Dua showed him his seat and explained something about a traditional ten minute grace period they accorded themselves. Ter checked the volume of the recessed desk mikes as Belem said he was usually the guilty one. "You know, the mañana mentality," he said, mimicking the cliché gesture of effusive Latin apology.

"It's not *farniente* that retards Sal," Sort winked. "It's his agrobusiness on other floors.

The Muscovite smiled politely and said he had heard about that. Belem looked heavenward in a gesture of mock repentance.

The noise of voices increased as the door opened and Soong Ast almost fell into the room, pursued by the reporters and their cameras on sticks. Nobu steaded the colonist and the two guards outside pushed back the newspeople. Nobu closed the door and Ast advanced with regained dignity.

"I didn't know they could be that persistent," the colonist smiled nervously.

"What do you want," Sort said. "You're a star!"

Ter wasn't sure she was supposed to overhear such talk.

"I thought stars were treated with extra respect," Ast smiled coming forward.

She still couldn't believe it! Above her sat chairman Nagpur and the twin cylinders' Ast was now less than two meters from her. She hadn't been to the colonies yet, but she had seen enough video. Each of the twin cylinders was twelve kilometers across and sixty kilometers long. They rotated slowly in opposite directions once every two minutes to provide normal gravity. There were large mirrors outside to reflect sunlight through the kilometer-long panels onto the land areas and the cylinders were surrounded by rings of small agrounits. You docked at the north pole and inside forty million people lived under clouds and a blue sky in cities and parklands.

She found Ast like most visiting colonists—bland and intelligent, with his uncertain skin color. Full gravity did something to their complexion. He was tall and, she had to admit, he was nice-looking in his tailored Unisave garb. She could understand why women were supposed to run after him. He would have to be about the only twenty-eight-year-old who wasn't on inhibitors. After all, how many colonist gynecologists under thirty were visiting earthside at one time. But she couldn't conjure up any video gossip of Ast with any famous Manhattanites, except Tina Dua maybe. The clip that came to mind was Soong Ast with his pretty mission deputee, who was also a second generation colonist. Zad something was her name.

Sort introduced Ast to their new colleague.

Mag said that despite all the lolling about in low g swimming pools that colonists indulged in, they weren't half as interesting as mature earthies. It was something about stamina; colonists were pooped faster. Mag should know.

She watched the others. She wanted to be able to give Mag a description of what they really looked like tonight. She'd be terribly jealous. Mag had four years' seniority over her but she had never worked Unisave.

"Yes, I plan to go home this weekend," Ast told Lim and Sort. "It's my mother's birthday."

"My wife plans to come over next week to begin looking for an apartment. I understand . . ."

"Good luck," Tok interrupted.

But Belem suggested Bo Lim's wife get in touch with Viv Bord or Tina Dua.

"Yes, Misha told me Mrs. Dua might be helpful," Lim said, turning toward Zeke.

They were interrupted by new commotion outside and all looked toward the door as Nobu smartly opened it. Surrounded by camera poles and newspeople falling over each other, Iyabo Att stood in the doorway.

She was in full UNCTAD robes. Almost unconsciously, the men all rose as she came in with a regal smile. Behind her the guard battered back the media people and managed to close the door.

"Iyabo," Jammu said, stepping down from his podium and crossing to greet her.

Ki thought the Nobel prizewinner was irresistibly beautiful. Her robe was azure with gold bands on her arms and it reached to the floor. The headscarf was lavender with geometric designs in red and when she moved the golden sleeves fell back and revealed a zigzag bracelet. The chairman led Iyabo toward Lim for a formal introduction.

"I'm so sorry you're not a woman," Iyabo smiled to the Muscovite.

"Misha sends her regards," Lim managed.

Iyabo turned from Lim to Dua and, after they exchanged an affectionate peck, she held Belem's hand for a long moment.

"You look extraordinary," the Brazilian complimented her.

Iyabo smiled. "The recess seems to have agreed with all of us."

Reluctantly, the general let go of her hand and she went to the seat on the opposite side of the horseshoe, putting a hand on Tok's shoulder as she passed him, nodding again to Lim, and offering her chin to the colonist who stood up to greet her. Their kiss was the merest of touches.

Ter watched Iyabo's voice level as the UNCTAD delegate sat down and kept talking with Ast on her right. The needle showed Iyabo was a little nervous.

The delegates smalltalked around the horseshoe. Ter balanced the levels for the master and felt a new tingle of pleasure. She didn't have the seniority, yet here she was, sitting under chairman Nagpur and balancing the voice levels of the Unisave seven. She'd call her parents tonight, maybe even her grandmother. She looked up at the chairman and decided he looked like the worldly-wise Urdu he was, the person who inspired confidence and wisdom in people in all ecosystems. His eyes were piercingly black but softened by long eyelashes. His mouth was sensuous, his nose commanding, but it was the deep, deep eyes that dominated his face. People named their quotas after him. She might want to do that herself one day although she wasn't sure she'd want a child in the present climate. Kids were just about the last thing the planet needed! Anyway, a mate came first and judging by the kind of guys just off inhibitors that Mag had introduced her to lately, it didn't seem mating was imminent for her.

She leaned her head on her right hand. She was ready. The chairman talked with UNCTAD's Iyabo Att on her right. He was a bachelor and a former videomaker who had once produced UN docus on population care. She swiveled on her chair and watched him. She noticed his uniform, probably of silk or some other ancient fabric. It was appropriate that Asia, the largest system, should be represented by Jammu Nagpur, that he should be chairman and that he should wear a uniform made of venerable material.

Jammu was a fused Asian, they said. He was pragmatic and irreligious like a premordial Chinese, theoretical and vaguely religious as an Indian of yore, sensitive and passive like a Laotian, rash and creative like an ancient Korean. She didn't believe any of that, but she felt a twinge of jealousy. Tokyo had been part of Asia once. The Hundred and Forty confederation had never been populous enough—thank God!—to rate a Unisave seat. Her system's only claim to Population Care fame was Tsu Egi.

Iyabo Att listened to the chairman and nodded. Ter wondered how UNCTAD women managed to fashion those magnificent scarves around their heads. She watched Iyabo's long folded hands and looked forward to seeing how the widowed scientist would handle debate. And she loved her accent, the hollow a's and the surprising lilt of her cadence. All UN secretaries were at least trilingual and Ter was very aware of speech and accents. In a homogenized world accents were the last delicious regional traces—her mother's singsong, Mag's native Manhattan twang, Sal's liquid r's and l's. She would like to visit Lagos, but she had promised Mag they'd spend their next vacation touring the Southcone. Of all the homogenized peoples, the Brazilians were the most beautiful—especially the men, Mag said.

Belem sat on her left next to Zeke. She watched him and decided he looked like a military person, although she had never seen one in the flesh. It was such a premordial profession. She remembered news clips of the civil war from her childhood, always the same scenes, it seemed. She could imagine Belem in battle fatigues. She could see him with a glistening face moving silently through unconditioned jungle with a drawn blaster, now and then slapping a mosquito from his chin. She had seen that in old video films.

She wondered if there was any rhyme or reason to the seating. Clockwise, it started with Zeke Dua on her left, then the general, Tok Sort who sat tipped back in his seat, the new Muscovite, Soong Ast and Iyabo Att. Were they seated alphabetically? Yes, by ecosystem: Amcan, Cono sur, Eurocom, Moscom, Space and UNC-TAD. Behind Belem, guard Nobu was getting ready to sit down. He pushed his service weapon from the side to the front of his tummy, sat down and tilted the chair back against the door. Funny position. Under the chair, she glimpsed books. Was he going to sit and read during the historic session?

While talking to Sort on his right, the Muscovite took a thin manila folder from his attache case and put it on his desk in front of him. She thought Lim looked brainy but naive, like Mag's last beau. Lim was telling the Eurocom delegate he had just met Misha Sev at her undomed country residence, but his hands didn't leave the manila folder. Was he afraid someone might snatch it from him?

It was funny to think Ast was a gynecologist. She would have thought all gynecologists in the colonies would be female, although she couldn't imagine why. She noticed his long, slim hands and asked herself if she would let him examine her, intimately. He looked worried and she suddenly felt sorry for him. Seniors were unfair when they called him the most hated man on the planet. His sanitation plan was perhaps necessarily harsh and, anyway, it was based on Unido projections. She could imagine kilometers of readouts and UIC terminal screens designing the fateful graphs. And there were an awful lot of old people. You didn't really see them in Manhattan because here, as in other systems, they preferred to live in their own environments, their own suncities. Her own grandparents on her mother's side lived off the Great Barrier reef and enjoyed things active people couldn't imagine. They were in Sydney and Manila twice a year but didn't miss beehives. Yes, she'd phone her grandmother tonight. They'd get a kick out of hearing she had worked Unisave today.

". . . declare open the four hundred and

seventeenth meeting," she heard Jammu Nagpur say above her. They all looked at her and for a second she was panic-striken. She flushed and pulled the minutes toward her.

"Let's have the minutes of the last meeting when Misha was with us," the chairman said.

"Yes sir," she stammered.

She read the minutes, gaining composure as she read about Misha Sev proposing campaigns for the voluntary sanitation of chronically ill seniors, about Sal Belem's amendment to extend this call for voluntary euthanasia to all terminal cases regardless of age, and Tok Sort proposing a vote to discuss these and other qualitative measures at subsequent meetings. The motion was carried, 4-3. The motion to adjourn was proposed by the chair and seconded by Belem.

She looked up and met Tok Sort's mocking eyes.

"Very good," he smiled, making her blush again.

She thought she saw Iyabo Att look sharply from her to Sort.

PART II

1

Mentally, Tok Sort blew Iyabo a kiss. She was cute like that, pretending to be jealous.

Jammu Nagpur spoke. "Perhaps we can be a little sparing on oratory," he said as the flustered secretary rolled the master. With a nod toward Bo Lim, he added that their new colleague had traveled overnight and perhaps needed to get acquainted before they plunged into headier debate.

"Thank you," Lim said, "but . . ."

"That is, unless you have a proposal," Jammu interrupted, looking directly at the Muscovite.

"I do," Lim answered self-consciously. "But perhaps I should wait."

"You have a proposal?" Belem snapped.

"An amendment."

Tok noticed that Lim was nervous and that his hand was on a manila folder in front of him.

The new Moscom delegate looked from the general to Jammu before he spoke. "As I mentioned to chairman Nagpur on the way in from the skyport this morning, Misha Sev briefed me thoroughly on the week's meetings prior to the recess six weeks ago. I believe I can say that Misha Sev enjoys the full support of her system. Day before yesterday she told me to extend to you her most cordial greetings and her regrets at not being able to join you."

"But if she enjoys total support why are you here?" Tok couldn't help asking.

Lim lowered his voice as he answered. He had replaced Sev apparently for one reason only—her age. Yes, his distinguished predecessor was fifty-one and the sanitation proposal demanded that life-and-death lottery be played at sixty. Had the colonies proposed that people gamble for their lives at the age of ninety or a hundred, the municipal leadership might have taken a different view. This of course was conjecture on his part. No one should read anything personal into what he was saying. Middle-age was simply, well, a sensitive issue and . . .

"I'm fifty-four," Dua interrupted. "In less than six years I will be playing colonial lottery."

Zeke looked with great dignity from the silenced Bo to Soong.

"And Zeke here represents the most youth-obsessed ecosystem," Belem interjected to overcome the discomfort.

Tok was touched. Belem was not a man of flattery.

The Muscovite looked genuinely apologetic. He repeated that his appointment reflected nothing more than his system's sensitivity to mushrooming. Nothing else should be inferred. As they themselves knew much better than he, gericide was a divisive issue.

"Precisely," the chairman said softly. "This is why we must be courageous."

Again, Lim could only apologize. "No one is irreplaceable. Why did Soong Ast replace Ken Wei two years ago?"

"You have done your homework," Tok smiled.

"It's in every yearbook."

Tok thought the new man had been well-groomed, perhaps better than any of them realized. Who was being trained in Strasbourg to replace him? His own appointment had been a compromise. Had they known back then that Unisave would take on its own life, Strasbourg would have appointed someone else, a demographer instead of a past-interpreter perhaps. He had won the appointment as the Eurocom delegate to the ZG conference in Mexico City. Eurocom had not been considered for charter membership of the new agency since the Asean federation had more population and the seven seats were to go to the seven most populous ecosystems. But he had introduced the notion that people shouldn't be counted in numbers only, that their culture, their history also carried weight. His argument had been dismissed as elitist by the Aseans but enough delegates had been flattered into believing their premordial culture had contributed as much as Europe's to planetary civilization to make Strasbourg and not Singapore the seventh member. But why shouldn't they train someone to replace him. He might get seafood poisoning or—have to resign. He looked across at Iyabo and heard her express the thought he was formulating. Ecosystems should indeed train replacements, she told Bo Lim. Belem agreed and revealed he had Nilo Dor ready to take his place anytime.

Tok hoped none of them underestimated their new colleague. Aloud, he said he was sure he expressed everybody's sentiment when he extended his welcome to Bo Lim.

"Thank you, Mr. Sort," the new man smiled gratefully.

"Call me Tok," he winked.

"And perhaps we can get a tribute to Misha into the record," Zeke said. Looking at the secretary as if to be sure her tape was running, Zeke proposed that a statement of appreciation and best wishes be sent to Sev. All agreed and Lim said he would personally telephone the message to Misha later in the day.

"Yes," Tok said, leaning forward in his chair with an impatient gesture. "If we can get this cub scout initiation over with, perhaps we can get down to business."

With a light tap of his gavel, Nagpur revealed that he and Zeke had run a number of statistical projections through Columbia University computers during the recess. "What we found is not altogether new or startling, but it may have a bearing on our decision," the chairman said, looking around the horseshoe. "We all know the world's population is aging faster than had been suspected and we know certain ecosystems are dipping below zero growth. We know old people are no longer a homogenous group, that they are divided into the 'young old' who are on this side of a hundred, and the 'old old' who are over a hundred and represent the only growing segment of the population. But I regret to say that the elimination of misformed newborns, as Misha Sev suggested the last time, or the euthanasia of all chronically ill will not amount to anything that can possibly prevent the collision between upward demographics and flat-out food ceilings."

The chairman looked at Soong, but the colonist remained politely silent.

Tok threw himself back in his chair. This was not his day. He looked across at Iyabo and suddenly found her stilted and self-conscious. Why this circus outfit? He felt impatient, with this committee, with himself. He felt impatient with the slowness of progress, the perpetual turnover, each generation painstakingly starting from scratch, Zeke's fretting about age, hungry kids moving up and sharpening their claws. He had asked Iyabo why we couldn't transmit just a wee bit more in those clever little DNA spirals. Why was it that just as he had managed the mechanics of living, his son and daughter would have to start the whole experience over again, all the adolescent traumas, the whole predictable repetition. Why couldn't knowledge be cumulative—men and women transmitting themselves whole at the moment of conception so their offspring could continue from there. Or just some knowledge. Like language. A kid can see and hear at birth, why can't he speak or count to ten? Why did it take thirty years to begin to draw unforeseen conclusions?

Iyabo had been cool and exciting that first afternoon. We're working at it, she had smiled and pulled him down to her on the bed. She and Tunde had received their Nobel medal for theoretical biology, or, as she had laughed, for finding out that biology and life had nothing to do with one another. She told him about cloning and other asexual reproduction. "Just think of hatching a thousand virtually identical Tok Sorts, a whole colony of darling Toks," she had laughed.

That was six weeks ago, a few days after the recess. He had called her office to apologize for some of his sarcasm leading up to the recess vote and they had met for coffee. It had been something new to meet outside the Unisave work-frame, outside the family ambiance of the Duas' Montauk weekends. Nobody questioned life in test tubes anymore, she had explained. The idea was no longer to grasp outlines, but to analyze systems of life, their structure and function. She had talked about her late husband, his great work. If you wanted to describe life, Tunde had discovered, you referred to its logic, to the way it was "made" as well as the way it reproduced itself and evolved.

He looked across at her and felt the knot inside him melt away. She had told him about her husband's last months, when his speech had been so badly affected that he used a special terminal keyboard to express himself. Tunde had worked at the Pasteur to the end, not so much pushing logic to the absurd as trying to make logic out of the absurdity of cellular life. Iyabo had revealed a side of herself he hadn't known. The next day he had found a pretext for inviting her to the penthouse restaurant in his building for lunch. It was all false lightness and clever repartee, joggling theoretical biology and past-interpretation to cover up silences and the absence of excuses to continue talking. The meeting ground had been social engineering, but he had sensed her willingness to surrender. Her reticence also, and he had imagined how it would be, infinitely disturbing, perhaps her first time in years with someone who was not a paraplegic. But it had been another three days, after another lunch at the penthouse, before he had invited her down to his apartment.

They had talked science and their overlapping disciplines, but they had both sensed it would happen. Past-interpreters had once believed history was linear and cumulative, one century neatly on top of the other. She had listened, sitting far from him at the window with the metal sky iridescent behind her head and figure. Just as living to be a hundred and eighty and living in space colonies had given people a new perspective and a new awareness, so standing room only had taught people metadetermination. That was the current view, he had explained. When the population reached twenty billion, governments, whether benevolent or dictatorial, had died because no one *could* rule. The wall of human flesh cancelled out all orders—and China had become the first nation-state to discover rule by osmosis. The laws of metadetermination had followed, planetary rule became self-evident, and the UN was resuscitated. But before that, past-interpreters had already caused the demise of Marxism. She knew that, but said she'd love to hear him tell it from his point of view. It was silly. Physics and mathematics discovered contingency, but Communists remained stuck between "anything can happen" and "only what Marxist-Leninism says can happen." It was dumb, especially after past-interpreters had applied contingency to history and discovered that history was nothing more than a series of improbable states, something like playing roulette. Your number will come up sooner or later. The *only* unknown factor is how many spins of the ball it takes. Chance, therefore, was only momentary. And in history, as Tunde and Iyabo had discovered in microbiology, evolution was a series of improbable states.

History only made sense in hindsight. Who would have guessed that the whole-earth perspective would be the consequence of nation-states' no longer being able to afford both arms and food. As the last Marxist leader had told the last U.S. president, "What do you need nuclear warheads for? You've got soybeans!" World War III hadn't happened because nobody could afford it and because ultraintelligent computers made it clear all wars were equally stupid—you made war and (a) lost and went home, or (b) you conquered, stayed and (c) became a mixture of you and them. The civil war in the Southcone had been the exception, an intractable exception. It hadn't been particularly murderous; it had merely dragged on. It was the crunch of expanding population and finite biomass that had ended Marxism. Socialism had a way of loading the greatest technopol burden on the country that could least afford it. With the establishment of the first Barnal spheres and the realization that powersats beaming inexhaustible solar energy down on the planet could pay for space industrialization, the similarities among people began to stand out more sharply than their differences. "From a diverse past into a shared future," was the slogan of the twenty-first century, which had discovered that increased food was ultimately a trap since it merely invited more population growth. History was a crucial permanence.

Tok looked across at Iyabo and wished they were alone again. He had crossed to the window. They had watched the steel sky and he had touched her for the first time.

She was listening to Jammu, one hand on the

desk in front of her and the other under her chin.
The headscarf made her slender modernness
seem fuller and wiser. She had a way of feeling
her way into a situation that hadn't been spoiled
by her seriousness as a scientist. And as the
widow of a great men. He felt her premordial
dressing up today was more than a mood, more
than a compliment to him, or to their secret. It
was a sign, something more than morality and
sexuality. He loved the openness of her face and
felt a hint of guilt for forcing her to dissimulate.
It was so contrary to her bioethics. His own, too.

He heard the chairman say it had been exciting
to work with young mathematicians.

"Anything you can tell us?" Iyabo asked.

Jammu proceeded to give examples of the kind
of demographics he and the young mathematicians had run through the UICs. Illnesses and
loss of sensory perception rose steeply after a
hundred and forty. Only twenty persons out of a
thousand under a hundred lived in nursing
homes, but the figure rose to fifty-five in the
hundred-to-hundred-and-twenty age group and
to nearly three hundred in individuals over a
hundred and fifty. These stages posed important
questions of public policy. "How old is old," the
chairman asked significantly.

Tok had phoned Kikki this morning, but he
hadn't said anything. Ank had already been off
to school, but he had kissed Ise on the screen and
told them he'd come home next weekend or the
next. Kikki had talked about her grandparents in
an exasperating tone, as if to say that if he didn't
vote against gericide again, they would be the
first to go. Twice she reminded him of their
hundredth anniversary next year.

He looked at Bo Lim on his left, sitting with his hands on his manila folder. "Maybe Bo here should open his folder," he said.

But Zeke said he had a point of order question. If Bo Lim's envelope contained an amendment, he, Zeke, would like to say a few words on the original geriatric sanitation proposal before the committee.

"Anything new?" Tok asked.

"A plea for reason, for dignity and for compassion."

Tok smiled. "What we need is *imagination*."

The chair ruled Dua in order.

2

Soong Ast listened to Dua say that today's young were the first to realize that society was prefabricated, that their future was rigged. To be young is to think about the world you want to live in, Zeke said. As we grow older, we learn to narrow and interiorize our views. In adult life, the individual still has a century ahead of him to work for change. The hundreds are a time for interior growth of a kind former times never suspected, but in the last, last years the future is no longer there. Our existence is, after all, finite.

Soong felt Zeke wanted someone to challenge him—ardent pleas sounded better in the heat of give and take—but they all sat back, apparently ready to hear out their senior member. Soong leaned back and watched the ceiling paneling.

"You have to live a long time to be able to *foresee* the present," Zeke said in an impassioned voice. "Goya painted his most daring works after he was forced into exile at seventy-seven, Beethoven exceeded himself in his last quartets, Voltaire wrote *Candide* in his sixties, Sarah Akhmanova gained fame in her nineties only." Life would be richer, he continued, if a wider choice was encouraged throughout life. The greatest danger was to freeze people into roles that limited self-expression and development. During the last two hundred years, upward mobility, medical breakthroughs and homogenization had added eighty years to the average person's life. To life to be a hundred and fifty also meant you must flesh out those hundred and fifty years, that you must have something to do, to live for.

Soong listened with sympathy, but he knew Zeke would receive little more than polite nods. Earthsiders were set in their ways and not moving with the times. It struck him again as he listened and let his eyes wander around the horseshoe. Zeke was pleading for dignity, but overcrowding cheapened life. Even famous and adulated men and women never felt satisfied, Zeke said. Life was never a serene look over the shoulder at accomplishments but a peevish glance at missed chances, at a past lying frozen and unchangeable behind you. The early colonies had been strongly tied to earth and governed by considerations of economy, by how much energy they could sell back to the planet. Barnal spheres had built powersats which had assured material wealth on earth and an inexhaustible supply of resources which in itself had promoted the conditions for zero growth. Except for the growing old age mushroom, Soong thought. The irony was that the colonies needed earth less and less while earthside ecosystems needed the colonies more and more for the sense of purpose and perspective that the high frontier offered the beehives and Zeke's centenarians looking for self-expression and development.

He thought of home. Under an undomed sky, home was minus 65 degrees declination and 15 hours ascension on the Mercator map of a starry night. It was out toward Alpha Centauri, but only eighty millionth of the distance to the star. By ion drive cruiser it was two hours away and by a new fusion ship a minute and a half, although of course no starship could reach top velocity and decelerate on such a short hop. By shuttle his happy valley was two hour's from Zad's home colony and four and a half hours from the twin cylinders of the municipal council. They were twenty million in his colony, spread sparsely over the hundred kilometers of the torus' circumference. Planetary chauvinists talked about the beauty of the oceans, the mountains and the sweeping plains, but all humans down here lived in domed beehives since Unido had made all agroregions off-limits and people only knew of oceans, mountains and plains from century-old video clips. On his torus, as he had told Zeke's wife, you could stand on your verandah and look over fields and forests toward the horizon curving up and out of sight and coming back far behind you in the same gently bending perspective. Or you could look to the side through the continuous panels of windows and see the majesty of space, the unutterable sideral vastness that provided the theme and inspiration of so much colonist art. Slowly, you would comprehend that colonists were people of space. Later perhaps, an hour later, perhaps a year later, you would understand that space was the logical habitat, that planets were poor places to live. Planets had high gravity which made it hard to get down to and off from their surfaces. Gravity interfered with heavy construction and getting around, and in a deeper sense prevented flights of the imagination.

He listened to Zeke and felt the problem facing the seven of them shrink inside him. To shake himself out of his reverie, he leaned forward. His foot accidentally kicked the metal wastepaper basket under his desk, making Bo Lim next to him turn for a second. Leaning on his elbows, Soong thought it was all pretty simple; a solution tended to emerge from the mere raising of the issue itself. Geriatric sanitation was the last draconian measure man must take against his own expanding—and aging—flesh. For seven years now, Unisave had finetuned its basic rule of zero which said every human being could replace himself but only himself, meaning that each couple could have two children. Unisave had forbidden marriage before thirty and made sterilization compulsory after forty-eight regardless of whether you had used up your quota or not. Young people were on sex suppressants and beehive apartment buildings were under electronic surveillance to discourage promiscuity. And all this was symbiotic and metadetermined. People didn't feel oppressed—if anything the basic rule of zero was recognized as one giant leap up from a hideously anarchic past.

Zeke said it was best to accept what you couldn't do anything about. "Psychology teaches us that to accept our shortcomings makes us better human beings. If the aging man and woman can have no other goals, they can try to accept what tends to diminish them—age."

Zeke knew how to be eloquent, Soong thought.

"Last night, President Hoo told me the noblest role of age is an affirmative one. It is to be an example. 'I'm still making progress,' Renoir said the day before he died at seventy-eight. Akhmanova tells us her paintings are now forty minutes long, that her work has never been stronger, nor more opulent."

Soong thought of his mother's own art. She would be sixty on Sunday and was just beginning computer artistry. Her latest work was ten minutes long. The drawing began with a diagonal, an emerald line that she let continue diagonally across the screen to anchor it to a dissolving background of magenta and purple. She added white brushwork and let the depth of field loosen itself in a receding perspective that turned on its axis. The yellow horizontal plane ebbed and she added a sideral night above it, tied the abstraction with jade greens and blacks that trickled like water and flooded the whole left side with a scarlet mass that spread with majestic calm and gave the whole enhancement a strange seductiveness. At the end, she dipped into the past and added Van Gogh's drawbridge and, over the night, hung orange, red and green circles like premordial lampions. Blue collages came last as the perspective turned on itself.

She had stood back with him, let the enhancement glow on the wallscreen and told him that visual inspiration didn't depend on her understanding it. He had promised himself—not her—he would try to be back on Sunday. Yesterday he had asked Zad to coordinate a shuttle from the twin cylinders to his home torus, and before going into session this morning she had confirmed the arrangement. His mother told him computer enhancements killed time and that they gave you new insights since you could recall all art that ever was and overlay it with its synthesis and your own imaginings.

He became aware that Zeke was no longer speaking, but looking across at him.

"The colonist proposal is momentuous for us," Zeke said. His words were measured and his voice solemn. "Until seven weeks ago our mandate was to control procreation, which meant our concern was men and women between thirty and forty-eight. With his proposal, Soong has made all people our concern."

Zeke let his glance travel around the horseshoe. Passionately, he added, "If all men are our concern today, the question is surely not only what the aged can do for society, but what society—Unisave—can do for them! If we are to try and find the solution, we cannot isolate ourselves from understanding our older selves, the people you and I will be in a hundred years. We, too, will be what they are."

Zeke let his words sink in. Again his gaze came to rest on Soong.

"We should have the imagination to change things," Zeke continued. "We should have the imagination to make life more than it is. We cannot sit back and accept that famine is inevitable in ten years, even if it is. We are not here to understand the inevitable, we're here to challenge it!"

The room was silent.

Soong thought that once you accepted Population Care, geriatric administration wasn't that farfetched. That, at least, had been the premise they had worked on during the elaboration of the proposal in the twin cylinders. If you believed in zero growth, geriatric care was the obvious flipside to birth management, the logical next step. He respected Zeke's indignation and tried to understand. The only offhand explanation that came to mind was that birthrates in the colonies were low—and the classical explanation for *that* was the continued immigration and the sense of a different adventure in space. Perhaps there was some subterranean variance of perception he didn't grasp.

Jammu spoke. "Self-knowledge is the beginning of wisdom, and it is the beginning of transformation and regeneration within ourselves. Perhaps if our forefathers had had a little more foresight . . ." He didn't finish his sentence.

"The enemy is our fathers' spermatozoa," Tok smiled looking at Iyabo.

Soong thought he saw Iyabo redden next to him, but Zeke brusquely leaned forward to let the attention focus on him again.

"I know that in a world governed by symbiosis and social design," Zeke said, "it is heresy to say this: but I don't think we have to *earn* the right to exist."

Soong was offended. As much as he had respected Zeke's defense of the aged, he felt irked by this blatant overplay. The idea of the individual not owing anything to society was insulting and undermined Dua's plea.

"You are inconsistent," Soong couldn't help saying. "On one hand you claim the individual doesn't owe society anything and on the other hand you say society owes the individual a dignified and enriching old age."

Iyabo spoke for the first time. They had to be practical, she said. There were a hundred newspeople out in the hall. Some sort of answer would have to be formulated. Do we institute gericide or don't we? Personally, she didn't feel anything new had been said, but the question was not what she felt but what the world expected. Their basic rule of zero worked not because the seven of them were the world's conscience or because they had engineered vast social changes. It worked because it was reasonable. "I agree with Tok that chronically ill old people should perhaps be terminated instead of being wheeled to a lottery station and I agree with the suggestion of euthanasia of all chronically ill people, but it won't work."

She looked from Zeke to Jammu as she reminded them of Sal Belem's argument six weeks ago. Like conscription, Sal had said, gericide had to be universal. She wasn't so naive as not to know that sons of powerful men had sat out premordial wars behind cozy desks, but the principle of universal conscription had been maintained.

"I forgot that," Sal smiled across to Iyabo.

"Whatever we decide—and we cannot express metadetermination since the metapolls are split right down the middle—it must be cleancut and without exceptions," she said. "It must be like molecular mathematics; it works because it's simple."

"You had us amend the basic rule to allow half quotas for individuals marrying divorcees with offspring," Zeke reminded her.

"Iyabo's right though," Tok cut in. "You can't be a little bit dead."

Iyabo nodded. "Even Misha admitted that simplicity was the major virtue of the colonist proposal."

Soong felt they all missed Misha, her brash, sandpaper voice and her instinct for bulldozing through cant. Anyone looking into protein synthesis or geodesic geometry, Iyabo continued, would have to admire nature's elegant simplicity. Their second rule would simply have to be as basic as their first.

After a silence, Tok said that the point was not the justice of universal draft laws or the beauty of molecular creation. "This is death control," he said a little sharply. "We must face up to gericide for what it is—extermination, not metaphor or statistical projections."

The colonies had suffered accidents on the way to the high frontier, Soong thought as he listened to Tok. Radiation shields had been invented through trial and error, meteoroid hazards had never been totally eliminated. Once every few years a torus was hit by meteorites large enough to break panels or punch holes in the hull but the colonies were so big now that when a panel was broken, it would take six hundred years for the air to leak out.

Tok said they shouldn't fall into the trap of believing that what is merely dramatic is there-

fore important. A thousand people dying in a
subsonic crash always appeared more important
than the death of a thousand people in modest
groups of twos and threes, in ground car mishaps. The important thing to grasp was that the
learning process was already beginning to take
effect. Less than zero growth already existed,
and negative growth was also incremental; it
also added up. And the high quality of life Zeke
wanted already existed.

"But as you say," Iyabo interrupted, "you
can't be just a little bit dead. Gericide *is* death
control."

They were going around in circles, Soong
realized.

3

After the short midafternoon break, Bo Lim
opened his manila folder and declared his
ecosystem was formally proposing the adapta-
tion of gericide with the proviso that couples
with over-sixty parents and grandparents could
prevent the elimination of their kin if they voluntarily abstained from having children as long
as their elders were alive. Two sixty-year-olds
minus two nonborn grandchildren equaled zero.

Even Jammu Nagpur smiled.

Tok Sort was the first to speak. It was fabulous,
he said, and so beautifully Russian.

"And eminently fair," Bo allowed, almost
jealous of Sort's enthusiasm.

It was something none of them had expected and the reaction was effusive. The chairman leaned on his elbows and curled his arms and hands around each other with visible pleasure. Iyabo leaned forward to smile to Bo. Tok threw himself back in his chair in an eloquent gesture of excitement and Sal grinned and slapped his desk as if to say, Why didn't I think of that one? Soong wrinkled his handsome brow as if doing a quick doublecheck. Even the little secretary felt free to smile.

"Simply beautiful," the general chuckled, shaking his head in mock disbelief.

Zeke almost had tears in his eyes and immediately stumbled on the obvious next step. "I'd go even further," he said. "I'd suggest that childless people be exempt from colonist bingo altogether. If you haven't replaced yourself why should you be asked to die for other people's offspring?"

"Thinking of Tina and yourself?" Tok asked.

Bo basked in the glow and thought of what Misha had told him about the profound pleasure of feeling the house of cards of diversity synergize into steely agreement.

"Two sexagenarians minus two nonborn grandchildren equals zero," Zeke repeated.

Iyabo was the first to say Bo's amendment was something she could vote for—with reservations.

Bo looked at her. "What reservations?" he asked anxiously.

Since they were talking about fairness, she said, she had to point out that gericide with a proviso for voluntary abstention would only be just in the future when a whole generation had

had a chance to exercise their choice. Today, it was arbitrary. Some people had procreated, others, like Zeke and Tina—and herself, had not. To make the amendment retroactive and simply begin the program next January 1, say, and give everybody a chance to delay having families as of that date until after their parents' natural demise would be the best they could do.

"And what about newlyweds *without* living parents?" Sal asked theoretically.

"Same as what I said," Zeke answered. "They'll be exempt just as sexagenarians without children."

"Something like that," Iyabo agreed. "Those with no living parents can go ahead and have their quota."

Bo noticed she tried to catch Tok's eyes.

Tok leaned forward again. "The only positive side effect I can see is that parents will start being nicer to their kids. Can't you see it? Dirty old millionaire bribing his daughter-dear to keep capsulating."

"What about rotten kids blackmailing their parents?" Zeke wondered. "I can think of more than one society heir threatening to knock up a ladyfriend unless the old man hands over the loot."

Bo laughed along with the others. What people would think of. When Lo Hals and he had gone over it the last time, none of them had thought of these kinds of things.

"Will you care to elaborate?" the chairman asked him.

Lim outlined the details. It would be a little complicated since each human being had two parents, four grandparents and eight great grandparents. A couple had eight grand-parents—the husband's paternal and maternal grandfathers and grandmothers and the wife's complementary foursome. Since everybody went off inhibitors at age thirty, each couple of quotabearing age had three-point-nine living grandparents. "Beyond the legal limitation, our bioethics people are of the opinion that voluntary abstention will further lower birthrates," he said, looking up from his folder.

"You mean much lower than zero?" Zeke asked.

"Voluntary abstention will instill the idea that your quota is begotten at the expense of someone else," Bo smiled.

Soong looked at him.

"What do you say, Soong?" Sal asked.

"I think we should let Bo Lim finish before we comment," the colonist said without betraying any emotions.

Bo remembered what Misha had said about the Brazilian, about his wonderfully alert sense of possibilities. Voluntary abstention, Bo continued, was of course based on the backup penalty of gericide and, as such, was nothing more than an amendment to Dr. Ast's proposal tabled at the one thousand four hundred and sixteenth meeting seven weeks ago.

"Well, well." Tok rubbed his hands energetically. "Makes you feel you're really here for something."

As chairman Nagpur reformulated the amendment in Unisave's own parliamentary language, Bo watched his new colleages. They were more interesting than he had thought, less reserved, even if Dr. Ast and the chairman really hadn't said anything yet. He liked Zeke for his compassion and understood why Misha had told him to follow the Amcan delegate if in doubt. Sal Belem was the kind of person nobody wanted as his enemy and he imagined Iyabo Att could be intimidating.

He thought Lo Hals and the presidium had acted wisely. It sounded silly but Misha was jaded, as if she had seen it all too many times. She had told him things he had not yet sorted out in his mind. Before he had hopped back into the hover, she had hugged him. It had been embarrassing, in front of the hover pilot. Just day before yesterday. She had given him sketches of his future colleagues, and cautioned him that Unisave was not a cowboy movie with good guys and bad guys. Sitting opposite her visiphone that never rang once during the afternoon, she had said that his sudden appointment should make him suspicious of his own system. Lo Hals was a brilliant bioengineer and she was flattered to see one of Hals' collaborators take her place, but perhaps Bo should wonder why Moscow had seen fit to make him take over from her on such short notice.

He had followed Hals' suggestion and tactfully avoided telling her the truth. They had walked along a hedgerow and there was indeed no reason to hurt her. It had looked like rain and since he had never experienced an unconditioned sky, she cut across a field and along the next agroplanning field of biomass. He followed her, thinking she treated him with the negligent kindness you reserve for a grown son to whom, against your better judgment, you have to relinquish your enterprise. When he told her that she smiled for the first time. She asked about his wife and he told her Dra and he had their two quotas, two girls, and that Dra would follow him to Manhattan next week.

"It's hard to find a decent apartment."

"So I hear."

"Get to know Tina Dua; she knows a lot of people."

Misha had never asked him what he thought of gericide, thereby sparing him the embarrassment of having to lie about voluntary abstention. She had told him to look for an apartment outside mission channels in any case because Manhattanites were blasé when it came to delegates and technopols. When he asked what she would do now, she said "Walk in the fields and watch the biomass grow." Also, she would work on a revised edition of *Population Cycles*. Now that UICs were in charge of medical technology and had reached the point where their intelligence expanded exponentially, her book was hopelessly outdated. "It's hard not to sound sensational about this, but it's a sensational concept—UICs, not my book, that is."

He had been nervous under the sky that threatened to become wet at any time. Misha had outstanding invitations to lecture in a half dozen cities, she said. At her dasha they walked past the parked hover and the smartly uniformed pilot. The man just looked at them as they crossed the small lawn and she showed him how to scrape wet earth from his shoes. It was the first time a hover had been put at his disposal—since the ceremony in the morning everything had been VIP—and on the way back he had talked too much. He knew it was better to sit back in icy silence, that the pilot didn't care anyway, that to him it was all in a day's assignment, chopping one Bo Lim from old Bykov U to Kalinin outside the dome and back. A week ago, he had been a bioengineer synthesizing ammonia with bacteroid nitrogenase, a bioengineer, they said, with a brilliant future. His hunch was that rhizobium bacteria could fix nitrogen in soybean root nodules without the waste of hydrogen. Now, genes responsible for nitrogen fixation could be introduced into a plasmid and the cloned DNA bacteria endowed with nitrogen-fixing capability. It was not considered likely that such genes could be introduced directly into plant cells, at least not for several years, but when they could—goodbye Unisave, hello Unido! In that case voluntary abstention would be a stopgap measure, if ever there was one, since food production would double and maybe double again. As he had told Hals, he was happy with the appointment—it was an honor and a welcome change of pace, as things stood—but he sure wanted to be back in his smock before they unveiled the superplant.

When the rain started he had asked Misha if they could go to the back door and watch. He held out his hand and experienced the sensation of unconditioned drops falling on his skin. It was there that she told him to follow Zeke when in doubt because Dua understood the cost society paid when it neglected its members' self-interest. She had invited him to put on a pair of her boots and walk out in the drizzle, but he had felt that was too much and declined. During the break this afternoon, he had told Dua, Sort and Att about Misha's country home in unconditioned Kalinin, but he hadn't mentioned the rain.

He watched Soong Ast listen to Iyabo and realized that except for his brother-in-law he had never met a colonist this intimately, had never worked with one. Misha had made tea and told him Ast was born an old man. When he asked what she meant, she explained that Soong had never been young somehow, perhaps because he was born in a happy valley half a million kilometers toward Alpha Centauri, perhaps because he was so gifted he had never had a chance to be irresponsible. They had taken off their muddy shoes and he had watched the sinking sun peek through rain clouds and tried not to feel uneasy. As they sat in their socks, she had said there were two kinds of people—those who believed divine power had something to do with the whole thing, and those who believed man was alone and must have the courage to act despite almost certain knowledge he will make mistakes. Soong belonged to this second category—as she did herself. He had told her about his research, about the present understanding of gene structure and function. He also told her about introducing plasmids and what it would mean in food production five, ten years down the road. It had been like a premordial afternoon, sipping tea in the cottage while the hover stood outside in a soggy field. He asked if they shouldn't invite the pilot in, and she said he would have to learn to be arrogant.

In two days he would be in Manhattan, expressing the metadetermination of four billion Muscovites, she had said, but his job was not to defend his side against anybody. It was to seek the highest synthesis. In Population Care, progress was not in a straight line, but in the middle of a knot, like in a pretzel. There was no "up" in Population Care; progress was simply elsewhere. He had tried to compare Unisave's deliberations to the way nitrogen-fixing bacteria assimilated the ammonia into their amino-acid pools, in symbiotic associations controlled by enzymes. She had stopped him, saying she knew nothing about microorganisms, but that one of the greatest pleasures of sitting on a UN committee was to take part in creative synergy and feel the joint actions increase each other's effectiveness.

She had walked him to the hover and told him what she would regret most were the weekend parties that Tina and Zeke Dua gave every summer at a dasha that was actually an abandoned lighthouse on the former coast of Long Island. "When you get invited, you and your wife will understand what I mean." At the hover she added that the presidium could have been a little more delicate in easing her out. Hals could have told her a little earlier that she was a geriatric embarrassment. He hadn't had the heart to tell her a young delegate was a necessity since voluntary abstention would tend to deprive young people of their right to procreate. If presented by Misha, voluntary abstention would come off as another middle-aged ploy to screw the young.

4

Jammu Nagpur steered the debate toward consensus, but Sal Belem argued that if the children of a sexagenarian bingo loser refused to abstain, a local Population Care board had no other choice but to enforce sanitation.

"But how can you make one person responsible for someone else's life," Tok interjected. "Nobody is his brother's keeper, let alone his grandmother's."

"But voluntary abstention must be backed up," Bo Lim reminded him.

Tok was back. "You can't make one human being's life depend on the goodwill of another . . . what am I saying, make one person's life depend on the goodwill of a *pair* of others. Suppose a newlywed bride doesn't mind waiting until her grandma dies, but the groom has no living parents and can't see why he should wait?"

"A child is always a joint responsibility," Iyabo smiled across at Sort.

"Sure. But while you and I fight a paternity suit in court, the little thing is alive and kicking. In fact, it doesn't matter whether you and I agree to be responsible, *its* life is not endangered."

Jammu watched Sort and Iyabo and realized the rumors were true. The two of them were guiltily intimate.

"If we carry your argument to its logical extreme," Zeke intervened, "gericide won't be possible at all. How can you hold anyone hostage to unborn, as yet hypothetical, beings?"

Jammu wasn't sure he wanted to know about Tok and Iyabo. While he followed the pingpong of the debate, he watched them, she the Nobel-winning scientist who, with her late husband, had extended the bounds of knowledge by one step; Tok the self-assured, conceited and charming logician who knew he was brainy but was brainy enough to know when to make fun of his own superiority. A week ago, Jammu had received a long call from Iyabo. Now he realized the lonely faces she had talked about, the problems of morality that single women faced, were her own, that she had talked about herself all the time.

"It doesn't follow that my assertions are untrue just because they're inconvenient," Zeke answered Sal. "It does follow, as a practical matter, that these conclusions are appreciated by many who are capable of translating their appreciation into material support."

"But Zeke," Iyabo smiled, "we're not talking about private financing of new, enthusiastic studies about life after one hundred."

Jammu wasn't sure he could understand the motives that had made Iyabo and Tok lovers. He was often a fool when it came to perceiving the amorous undertow of other people's motives. Tok had always teased Iyabo, a gentle mocking of her scientist's innocence and sharp logic. It had started during the long debate on how to implement the basic right. Their first decision had been to simply give every newborn human being an extra digit in his or her Population Care magnetic tape. The moment a woman went to the hospital to have a baby—or even before, during pregnancy when she had her first checkup—the hospital administration deleted the digit in either the wife's or the husband's Population Care record. The extra digit was fair—as long as people didn't cheat. The trouble had started when Misha had asked what would happen if a divorced woman met a man who told her he was a full quota but actually had already used his digit? Iyabo had suggested they turn the planet into a matriarchy with women holding two digits in their PC records. This meant every woman could give birth twice regardless of who fathered the offspring. But planetary opinion hadn't liked the idea. There had been sick jokes in Strasbourg, stern moralizing in Ankara and quiet despair in Hundred Forty beehives. Tradition-oriented systems had sent in transcripts of local determination charts showing symbiosis would not be possible.

The "plugging of the loopholes" had actually taken years. Unisave had been obliged to create subcommittees of all kinds and illegal quotas had been Iyabo's specialty and Tok's inspiration for perpetual ribbing. One of their subcommittees still investigated transsystem infringements. This committee was the result of Iyabo's master coup: the uncovering of one Odessa resident who had pursued fullquota ladies in three systems, marrying them all and fathering six children. Dirty songs had been written until Unisave had hooked systemwide PC records together for a planetary master computer. One song stayed on top of the hit parade for one year in Tokyo and twenty-six weeks in Rio. There was even a saucy Muscovite version,

Misha told them, satirizing the "Seven ballcutters" in Manhattan. For the better part of one year, their debate had centered on the dilemma of divorcees with one child. At the end they had decided that if a pregnant woman appeared at a PC center and her record showed she was no longer a fullquota person, she could either pay a penalty or abort and face compulsory sterilization. Wei and Belem had been against this "premordial revival" of capitalism, but Misha had prevailed with an empassioned plea for victims of faithless men. "Are you saying a woman has to demand proof before she goes off her capsule," Misha had asked. "And how can she *ever* trust a man without access to his PC readout?" They had all realized that such instances were extremely rare. Sex was not fashionable and hundreds of millions of people remained childless. But the question for Unisave was not decimal points of bootleg pregnancies, but justice carried to its own logical limits.

Jammu looked from Tok to Iyabo and back again. He could imagine the pressure the two of them must feel. They were breaking all the rules.

"Well, let's not be naive," Tok said. "Geriatric sanitation is highly congenial to the economic interests of all systems. Forty percent of all expenditures go to the elderly and by the end of the century the share will rise to over half."

Zeke was impatient as he interrupted. "If we continue to see all seniors as inept and as a social deficit, we don't see the opportunities they offer—to themselves and to us."

An hour later they voted to go into a night session, over Jammu's objections. He and Zeke cast the nays, he because a night session might raise false hopes and Zeke because he said he was dead tired. As soon as the 5-2 vote was recorded, Tok said they might just as well decree lower-than-zero birthrates and drop the whole geriatric business.

"In that case," Jammu said with a quick bang of his gavel, "I'll ask for a vote on the proposal on the floor before we consider any new business." He was upset. Besides the false hopes, he said, there was the temptation of the mediapeople in the hallway during a dinner recess.

"This is the most vulnerable moment," he said gravely. "Any leak will be catastrophic."

Sort spoke calmly but with an edge of impatience. "I don't see why you're so scared of the media, Jammu. We've just voted for a night session, which is an indication that we think we're getting somewhere."

"I agree," said Belem.

Sort said there was no reason they couldn't agree not to talk to any newspeople during the dinner break, nor was there any reason they couldn't forego dinner altogether. They were always talking about their noble role, maybe this was the moment to practice a little self-sacrifice and not to absolve themselves of responsibility for the breakdown in public confidence that pussyfooting would inevitably bring about. As for those who were too tired, Tok continued, looking pointedly at Zeke, modern pharmacology had invented an extraordinary assortment of stimulants.

"You are new here, Bo," Sort added, looking sternly at the new member on his left, "but some of us have been here an awful long time refining the basic rule down to derestrictions for closed-

quota divorcees marrying full-quota persons.
Then one day Soong Ast proposed to match natal
control with geriatric control and by God if after
one week's debate we don't take a six-week recess to clear our fragile minds and to metadeter-
mine with our home systems. Then, on your first
day here, you come with an amendment that
may be eminently sensible and by God if our
chairman doesn't suggest we suspend debate
lest the media begin to speculate we're up to
something."

"All right," Jammu smiled.

"All right what, Jammu?"

"You win."

"Win what, Jammu?"

Jammu suppressed a flicker of anger. "When I
mentioned the media, I meant we should try not
to dash any hopes in case we don't institute
voluntary abstention. I didn't realize we felt
so, so unanimous."

"You mean you don't trust any of us over the
threshold," Sort came back, nodding toward the
door behind him.

"If you want to put it that way—yes."

"What really hurts," Sort smiled, "is that
you're not necessarily wrong, Jammu."

Belem suggested they march up to the delegates' cafeteria in one group and stay together.
Bo nodded his assent and Belem said they could
have a screen put around one big table and eat
together.

"Let's not get too dramatic," Zeke drawled. "I
would like to get a bite to eat and one of those
wonder pill Tok suggests for tired blood, and I
promise I won't talk to any of those nasty newspeople in the corridor."

"What about not talking to your staff?" Iyabo asked.

Jammu steered them back to the issue at hand. "The idea that each human being is born at the expense of someone else can have farreaching consequences. If we don't want to make life a parody, we must make sure existing life is treated with respect."

"The right to live must be more important than the right to reproduce," Zeke said, looking around at the others.

When no one challenged him, Zeke said he agreed with Tok. They might just as well decree lower-than-zero birthrates because that was preferable to the suppression of any life. "To be human is to be unique," he added with dignity.

Tok smiled. "But that also means you're locked into your own self. You're you."

"I should hope so," Zeke answered.

Tok was patient. "But you're not any more anything when you're a hundred than when you're twenty."

"Nor am I any less anything!"

"Yes you are." Tok held Zeke's glance. "Most of your future is behind you; your past is a burden that can't be undone."

Jammu could feel the tension of age seep in again and thought of Rani Mazure at the end of her long life. She had died a few months short of her hundred and seventieth birthday. A year before that he had visited her, and she had told him that to reach supreme old age was to flow into the anonymity of life, to give up ego and self-assertion. He asked Tok if experience didn't make a difference between being twenty and a hundred.

"I guess in a few cases," Tok conceded. "A few exceptionally gifted people may develop skills over a lifetime that allow them to make rules out of exceptions."

Mazure had been so old that her own parents were born in the late twentieth century when the extremes met and extreme left and extreme right became the same thing. Jammu asked Bo Lim if there were any projections of what young people might do if they were actually confronted with the choice.

Lim opened his folder again. He had no hard figures, he said, but bioethics experts estimated a substantial number of young people would postpone having families.

Jammu watched the silent Soong Ast as they listened to Lim go into demographics. The colonist hadn't said anything yet. It was disturbing somehow, since the quality of life was such an important and beautiful tenet on the high frontier. The colonies had done so much during the past century to lift people's spirits, so much to make them seek the best in themselves. Not only had they helped their left-behind brethren to end the Malthusian crunch that for so long had perpetuated territoriality and war, but they had given earthsiders the prospect of an open system, indefinitely rich in future and adventure. Seven years ago, when the ZG conference had led to the creation of Unisave, people everywhere had wanted one of the seven seats to go to the colonies although extraplanetary humanity didn't exist in excess numbers and overpopulation was strictly a planetary problem. People had wanted a colonist on Unisave because the colonies were the focus of so many hopeful dreams, because to soar with ion ships, even if it was only on video, was to refuse the finite and predestined trend. Ken Wei had been an inspired first choice by the high frontier council.

5

Soong Ast listened to Lim's estimates of "persuasive discouragement" with flagging interest. He would have to get to his office, on whatever pretext, during the dinner recess and get Zad to call the council. There was no other way.

Bo Lim's idea was not repugnant to him. There was nothing wrong with voluntary abstention. Population Care had always stressed people participation and two children per couple had been the recommended limit in all systems for over a century. He found voluntary abstention ingenuous and appealing and was sorry to realize it wouldn't work. The numbers were totally wrong. He was sure Tok or Iyabo or someone else had also caught on and he only wondered why no one was saying anything.

He couldn't ask for an adjournment until tomorrow. As they said in medical school, the others would slaughter him with his own knife. Six weeks ago, he had used sarcasm against demands for a recess. Weren't they a fourth power committee, responsible to the General Assembly only?, he had jeered. That gave him another idea. If Zad couldn't get anyone on the twin cylinders, he could try Hibs.

He glanced at his digit and realized 0114 GMT wasn't exactly the best time for getting in touch with a high frontier councilmember who could advise him. The sanitation proposal had been metadetermined over months of twin cylinder coplanning and here he was trying to have his deputee call and insist that someone come up with a response while he was upstairs having dinner with his colleagues. How much time would Zad have—thirty, forty minutes, not counting the irritating four second roundtrip delay in hearing the other end.

Mentally, he began to formulate the question Zad would put to a councilmember. Would the council recommend a reversal if voluntary birth limitation produced equal results? He leaned forward and picked up a pen. His question would have to be precise if any number of colonies were to be queried and a symbiosis computed and relayed back in forty minutes.

Soong sensed Iyabo on his left watching his poised pen and he turned and smiled. Lim's amendment didn't mention anything about equal results, but that was understood—like estriol fluoridation. He had to laugh. He had invented theoretical fluoridation and dashed to St. Louis last night to test it on Egi Tsu. Now, Lim said voluntary abstention might cause *substantial* negative growth and Tok and Zeke suggested they might just as well order below-zero birthrates. So much for singular initiative. He should have consulted his staff last night, or Zad at least. Singular initiative was old-fashioned and deviant, and, obviously, non-productive.

There wasn't much chance of Zad's getting any councilmember. There wasn't even much chance that any councilmember could tell her what the colonies' posture should be if gericide was amended. The base of his stomach went tight and cold. To make decisions alone was not only premordial, deviant and nonproductive, it was the most difficult thing a colonist could face. At home, the sense of belonging was all-pervasive; no one was alone because no one could survive separate in space. It was something earthsiders didn't always understand despite the precedent of comsats. A kind of nervous system for the collective human race had grown out of the communications satellites. To know instantly what happened elsewhere was the first step toward belonging to a common future, toward realizing that global civilization was the sum total of all others. In the sideral vastness, clusters of humanity made fraternal interaction merge into a newer collective nervous system.

There was still Hibs Koa. But was the head of the colonist mission to the General Assembly available tonight? The Koas led busy diplomatic lives. Could Zad track him down?

He scribbled the note while Bo Lim summed up his system's demographic expectations. Should the colonies shift their position? That was basically the question. Should they back a voluntary system that wouldn't work, but might jolt enough earthsiders into producing nosediving birthrates that, in turn, might make a gericide less of a holocaust and more of a symbol? He watched Bo and wondered if the new Moscom delegate had been set up, whether he was a stalking horse for more important proposals. Bo was a bioengineer, not a gynecologist who'd shoot down his proposal in one second. Or a woman. Any woman would realize she couldn't postpone having a family too many decades or she wouldn't be able to have any children at all. If the thirty-year-old daughter of a sixty-year-old bingo loser were to wait until her father died at a hundred and sixty, she'd herself be a hundred and thirty. And no gynecologist would recommend childbearing much beyond sixty. It was absurd. Why wasn't Iyabo saying anything?

He put his note in his uniform breastpocket and watched the shy secretary. He sensed that she had understood because she didn't seem as interested as before. Committee secretaries usually had that glazed look that came with listening to endless debate they couldn't take part in, but this girl was alive and followed the arguments. At least she had been the last time he looked in her direction.

He regretted that voluntary abstention didn't work. It was simple and bioethical—your own mother or father, or grandmother etc., vs. and as-yet-unborn offspring. Moscom would be everybody's darling—for five minutes. He had never seen a Muscovite grandmother with shawl and boots like the little plastic dolls they sold downstairs in the gift shop and he had never known his own earthside grandparents. But if Bo's idea had worked, he would probably forego fatherhood himself. So would hundreds and millions of others.

PART III

1

No mediapeople—not even the smart guys who had scrambled upstairs to the cafeteria floor—got a word from the Unisave seven.

Jammu Nagpur told Patel Nobu to have security seal off a section of the restaurant and they marched out of the committeeroom in tight formation, Belem up front and Iyabo, trying to suppress a giggle, in the middle. The newspeople had sprung into action as soon as Nobu had stuck his head out and relayed the chairman's orders to the two guards outside. When the seven marched out, the newspeople were all over them, raining questions fast and furious, direct and insinuating questions in everything from Interlingua to UNspeak, tracking them with camerapens and recorders. But the seven walked past the increasingly stunned reporters and disappeared into a waiting elevator in ninety seconds flat. Nobu digited them.

In the elevator, Iyabo exploded into laughter. "Weren't we funny, marching down the hallway like that?"

"But it worked," Jammu smiled.

"Did you hear the lady asking if people will have to play bingo on odd or even days or simply on their sixtieth birthday?" Zeke asked.

"Somebody told me our night session has sent the Tokyo commodity market through the roof," Tok said.

Sal told them he had been asked if the Brazilian civil war veterans would be exempted.

"Why should they be?" Bo Lim asked, looking puzzled.

"Because they already faced death once, I guess."

On the penthouse floor they were met by Shi Kapoor, the maître d', who told Jammu everything was being set up in the old VIP lounge.

Security had extra men at the entrance. The move to the lounge foiled several video correspondents who were on first name basis with at least five of the seven and had found it clever to dash up here and see if they could get at least a hint of why Unisave was going into night session. As they walked toward the lounge, Iyabo saw Oti craning at the bar.

Inside the big lounge with its picture windows on the East River, the unit front melted away. Sal was met by Nilo Dor and immediately dragged his deputee toward the bar. Zeke went to the men's room while Soong Ast showed Lim the view of Brooklyn and the Long Island metal sky.

Iyabo stopped in the middle of the lounge. Seeing Oti had made her remember—and dismiss—Fagbure's dinner, but she wanted to be alone with Tok, if only for a little while. First, however, she wanted to get out of these ridiculous clothes. Her head itched under the scarf and she could think of nothing better than scratching her scalp.

"I think our chairman is worried." Tok was suddenly next to her and nodding toward Jammu, who eyed Sal and his deputee huddled at the bar with undisguised suspicion.

"Oh Tok," she sighed in a low voice. Waiters

were busy all around them, bringing chairs and silverware to the hastily set-up large table. One waiter was laying out a white tablecloth that was so big it touched the floor.

"We were supposed to have dinner—no matter what," Tok said with a gesture toward the table-setting.

"Dinner for seven," she said matter-of-factly.

Kapoor hovered over his waiters but she felt that the two of them were safe in the eye of the catering turmoil.

As if he read her mind, Tok winked and said Lim's amendment might be an aphrodisiac since it would introduce a notion of danger to uncapsulated sex, danger pleasantly once removed since it was your parents who paid.

"Danger is a stimulus?" she asked.

"Isn't it?" He looked at her.

They had always done it in the afternoon. It would be crazy any other time. How could either of them flaunt himself on the other's apartment visicheck? She had stayed until after dinner last night but she had been in his building since the afternoon. "I don't know," she smiled, "I almost envy those who can do it legally."

"Nice, yes."

She felt their minds were fumbling for a way to spend the night together.

"Maybe we should research this area," he smiled sexily. "Constitute a subcommittee of two and do field work."

"If we could travel, yes," she said dreamily.

"Maybe Soong can set wheels in motion for preferential emigration. Maybe we can go to one of those experimental rim habitats."

She looked at him. His smile was lingering on

his sensuous lips and she couldn't decide
whether he was kidding or hinting at a distant
solution. Settlers on rim colonies formed
specialized communities and developed syner-
getic ideals of how life should be lived.

"Or we can ask Zeke if he'll let us have the
western White House as a field center."

"Western White House?"

Waiters passed with glasses and silverware
and Tok turned slightly to look at Soong and Bo
at the picture window. A hover dropped into
view in preparation for landing on the auditorium roof below.

"On the Oregon coast," he added.

She remembered Zeke telling them about a
stretch of Pacific coast that he and Tina had
visited last week. "I've never been to a premordial place like that."

"Nor have I." He looked at her again, poised,
very close.

Zeke had told them how he and Tina had sat on
a sand dune and watched an unconditioned sunset. But Tok and she, too, had watched the sky
turn amber that first afternoon in his apartment.
The metal sky had been common, familiar and in
such contrast to the enormity of what they both
knew they were about to do when he zipped
down her tunic. A rim habitat sounded less
strange than a place with no humans, although
there was something forboding and exciting
about those few forgotten places where nobody
lived. To say something, she told him that parts
of the Kalahari Desert were like that, the
Seychelles islands, too. In premordial times,
couples who were not city dwellers or villagers

lived like that, in the middle of unconditioned biomass.

A waiter carried chairs past them.

"Sal says it's invigorating to sleep in nature, that recycled air has no resonance, no echo," she added.

They both glanced toward the Brazilian and his deputee at the bar. "He hasn't said much today," Tok said.

"Nor has our colonist."

Casually, Tok said there could still be fireworks. When she asked what he meant, he said he had an idea for a little psychodrama.

"Psychodrama?"

"Shake everybody up a little," he grimaced.

She smiled. At the picture window, Soong seemed to excuse himself from Lim. She, too, had to freshen up. The colonist walked toward the exit in his long cautious stride as if gravity still surprised him.

"Let's have a drink at least when it's all over," Tok sighed, looking at her.

Their faces were close. The two of them alone for a few days in an unconditioned place, with wind and maybe rain, wasn't repulsive to her. It reminded her of the evening at the Montauk light house two summers ago, when Tina had asked the men to light the fireplace. It was illegal, something she had only seen on video, people sitting and staring into flames, but Tina had a way of making the censurable appear racy and piquant. Tok, too, had that gift. She had had to go up and help Tunde change his bag, but she had smelled the fire all night.

"I'm glad we stopped biophilosophizing that

afternoon by your window," she said.

Mutely, Tok's eyes scrutinized hers with a lover's sweet anxiety. Then his lips curled into ironic affection. "Are all UNCTAD princesses mysterious and beautiful?" he asked playfully.

She smiled and said the dress was getting to be a bit much.

"Like the spice of night."

She felt her face redden and to distract him asked if he knew the legend of the rain queen. When he shook his head, she told him it was the tale of how the Kalahari Desert came into being. "I must tell you the story some other day," she teased.

"Why, is it that naughty?"

No, she smiled, it was the story of the Bantu king's daughter who bore a son although she was not married. "Her name was Mujaji. And the king threatened her for not telling him who had fathered her son. As a result, she stole the rain charm and the sacred beads and fled south with her son."

Their eyes met.

"The big Kalahari Desert is still there, undomed, since Mujaji left." She sensed he understood.

Quietly he said, "And I thought we had reached a ceasefire."

They were alone for a second. "Maybe I want you too much," she said, averting her eyes.

She saw Zeke come in, look around and notice them. With an effort, she caught Tok's glance and nodded toward the entrance to let him know someone was approaching.

"How about a drink, kids?" Zeke asked.

She excused herself, saying she would join

them in a minute. She was oppressively hot all of a sudden. She crossed to the phones, dialed her office and told Dosh to come up to the ladies' room with her makeup bag.

Dosh had to know where the bag was. "Where you did my scarf this morning." Dosh made her wait while she went looking for it. On a video screen next to the phones, a movie was interrupted with a news bulletin. An announcer cooed that Unisave was going into an extraordinary night session amidst reports that gericide was a virtual certainty and that a special report would follow these messages. The waiters were finishing setting up and Kapoor gallantly held a chair for Jammu at the head of the table. At the bar, Tok swung around on his stool and looked across the vastness of the room at her.

"I'll be right up," Dosh came back.

When Iyabo came back half an hour later with a fresh face and a newly-set headscarf, they were all at the table except Soong. Tok sat opposite Jammu at the other end of the table. She sat down next to Tok and began to listen to Lim describing Misha Sev's country place. Lim assured them their former colleague was enjoying her new freedom, that she took long walks in unconditioned nature, made tea in an ancient samovar and was going to revise *Population Cycles*.

"It sounds silly maybe," Lim said, stopping himself.

"Not at all," Jammu said politely.

She felt Tok's knee against hers.

Sal noticed she was back and looked at his digit with an impatient gesture.

While listening to Lim she moved her hand under the long tablecloth and along her thigh to the knees. After a long moment Tok's hand met hers. The grip was firm. Slowly their fingers interlocked. She told herself they were being careless, deliciously careless.

2

At the other end of the table, the chairman looked up and saw Soong Ast enter the lounge and come toward them.

"Let's order," Jammu said, interrupting Lim. With imperative gestures the maître d' distributed outsized menus, recommending the veal.

"Texturized?" Belem asked.

"The vegetables are organic," Kapoor smiled diplomatically.

Jammu watched Soong sit down. The colonist nodded an apology in his direction and picked up his menu.

"I only had two muffins this morning," Zeke announced, ordering the veal.

Kapoor hovered over Tok and Iyabo with his order sheet while Bo told Soong that he understood veal was something of an acquired taste for colonists. Soong explained that cattle were too wasteful in converting feed to protein, needing over twice as much intake as rabbits to produce a kilo of edible meat. Bo said his brother-in-law was a radio astronomer on a university torus in Jovian orbit, that he knew the most popular protein in research habitats was fish, grown in high humidity on special space farms where weightlessness prevented their gills from collapsing. Soong said his own colony grew a million fish like that in hundred percent humidity and politely asked what tract Bo's brother-in-law was surveying.

"Between two and four hundred lightyears out."

Listening for intelligent life among the galaxies was nothing new. Cyclops scientists cautioned against expecting prompt results—as they'd done for over a hundred years now—but every day another billion stars were processed. In another decade the Milky Way would be finished. The latest theory was that the meanderings of large ideas still defied the sharpest insights of the UICs or that all knowledge of a highly developed civilization could be contained in enormous, planetwide UICs that radiated no energy and therefore communicated nothing. Such a civilization would be a single organism where the essential of life—response to stimulus—was programmed and biological life was no longer necessary.

Jammu listened with detached emotions. He had seen Soong leave twenty-five minutes ago but felt helpless. Suppose the colonist had defied him? What could he do? Ask the guards to physically bar the exit? Like everyone else, he was moderately interested in the century-old search for intelligence, but at the same time he was impatient with speculation about what was out there. He could easily imagine a planet where the original biological creatures had given themselves over to ultraintelligent computers, since man was already so much the product of the knowledge and sensations of

UICs. But suppose the breakthrough proved how stupid we were? Suppose we received pictures of a thousand planets and every one of them was pockmarked by ruins of civilizations?

He ordered veal, shuddering at the vision of a million red snappers with gasping gills swimming, if that was the word, in zero g humidity. He had visited the twin cylinders once, in an official capacity, and resented the colonists' turning their backs on earth, their waterroom tissue attitude toward the planet—use it once and throw it away. For Soong, life emerged as a technical problem to which one responded with technical panaceas and socioeconomic solutions. He himself came from a region that was old, a system that had grown cautious because enthusiasm had been shattered many times and dreams had proved fragile. In his part of Asia, both the natural and human world were so prodigiously varied that to talk was often to say things that appeared to be the construction of extraordinary imagination. That was why he was melancholy sometimes—and cautious when it came to trusting people to be nobler than their motives. In premordial India, uncertainty had been the elemental fact of history, together with a deep awareness of past suffering. In premordial China, where he had deep roots from his mother's side, people were generally entangled in insoluble problems. Until homogenization, people in the eastern part of his system had believed society was imperfectible since man himself was imperfect. The colonies had done a lot to change that.

He noticed that the door was closed and two guards had taken up position, but he didn't like it up here. He wished they were safely back down in the committeeroom. The hiatus was dangerous; the pressure to speak was too great on all of them. And the opposite media pressure to find out was ever greater. That was why he had insisted on united silence. Thou shalt not tempt. But he could only demand this lockstep for a short while.

Kapoor took Tok Sort's order and disappeared. Jammu liked him. A good man, an Urdu who had been in UN service even longer than himself.

While they waited for the food, Zeke said the fiber muffins reminded him of an invitation Tina had told him to extend to everybody. It was for the tenth, for a theatrical evening. Tok perked up, but Zeke didn't know much about the play, except that it was avant-garde, twentieth century, about a couple going through a crisis with various risqué things happening. Bo Lim wanted to know if it had music in it; he had always wanted to see a classical American musical, live.

Soong accepted and entered the date on his pocket computer. He would want to see Mrs. Dua in any case, he said, about an exhibit of colonist art she had agreed to patronize.

"Computer terminal reveries?" Tok asked.

"Yes and no," Soong said.

Tok's voice was gently mocking. "Zoom-in on Michelangelo's David, naked, upright and vulnerable, until his left eye fills the visualizer and the sidereal black is cancelled by a fleeing horizon and its sinking sunstar is a glint on David's retina."

Soong smiled. "You'll see."

Jammu didn't really listen. This morning on the way in from the skyport, Lim had told him he

had only been to Manhattan twice before. They
were all so isolated, so helplessly unique, each
locked into his own self, as Tok had said. Lim
had only been to America twice before, he himself had never been married and knew he
couldn't understand what had driven Tok and
Iyabo to become intimate. Did Soong understand
ancient earthside reflexes? Could Zeke or Iyabo
imagine what it meant to grow up in an Asian
beehive? Could he imagine it himself? He had
grown up affluent and homogenized, the son of
a line of Madras videomakers, but it had taken
him many years to get rid of the guilt of
privileged birth.

He heard Soong order tea and Kapoor snap his
fingers and send someone off to the kitchen. Had
Kapoor grown up less than privileged? In Jammu's youth the nightmare of runaway population was still a living memory. His grandfather's
childhood had been spent hiding from hollow
eyes, bloated bellies and enfeebled brains. His
father's youth had been in the era when the subcontinent had traded its resources for food for
the last time, the last decades before powersats
had ended energy hunger. His grandfather on
his mother's side had known Manila spilling
into the South China Sea and his grandmother
had seen Nanking become a suburb of Shanghai.
When his parents first left the subcontinent they
realized the plight was largely self-inflicted, a
discovery that had made them and a billion
others hate nationalism. It was the year the subcontinent had suppressed flies and dogs, his
mother always remembered. Former centuries
had imagined that a world population of twenty
billion would lead to nightmarish dictatorships

when in fact it had led to total consensus. Old India had been the prime example. Its population had been so big that no one ruled and everything had become metadetermined and coplanned. It had struck him again during his last visit. On the lowest demographic level, Delphic polls suggested people's own sense of the future, overnight Arbitrons fine-tuned consciences. Social planners had shown him crisis centers for dissenters, and goals parliaments and ethics courts where decisions and judgments were interacted just as in the UN.

The dinner was served while Tok maintained that the greatest contribution of colonist art was its effort to express cosmic loneliness. Soong corrected him, saying that the effort was to express not loneliness but the search for an end to cosmic solitude.

Tok smiled. "If you can't have eternal bliss, long suffering at least adds up to a density."

The search for extraplanetary life brought Bo into the conversation since his brother-in-law was part of the Magellan program.

Jammu ate in silence, thinking Tok was probably right. Radio astronomers had been tuning in on the universe for two centuries, every so often announcing they were narrowing detectable civilizations down to less than ten thousand lightyears away. Maybe it was part of a premordial urge to last forever.

"Repentance must be just about the only emotion the artist can't feel when he looks at his visualizer," Tok said.

Jammu felt his apprehension subside with the texturized veal, the tea and the conversation. The dinner was conciliatory. He was glad the talk was about art because he feared the lounge might somehow be bugged by some of those enterprising newspeople. He thought of Rani Mazure. The late ZG president had called her own contemporaries "the terrible generation" for failing to see that demographics was the central issue of modern man. Would future generations call *them* terrible because they didn't have the courage to solve longevity, or the consequences of longevity?

"Art is always a series of questions, not a series of neat answers," Soong objected.

"Great art belongs to its time but it also escapes it," Tok said.

Jammu let the tea soothe his insides. They had also had tea three months ago when Soong had called and told him the colonies would propose gericide. Soong had gone through channels but hadn't said why he wanted a private late-evening meeting, and it had taken him an hour of cursory talk before coming to the point. Longevity and protection from disease can no longer be considered a total blessing, Soong had begun. Colonist agroplanners had detected that earth-side population and biomass were on a collision course, that they would impact in nine, ten years. Perhaps more important, euthanasia would be tolerable because the interest in longer life was waning, even in global standard systems. The solution suggested itself—random elimination of one third of the excess load. There was no doubt geriatric sanitation would be metadetermined to show it was an idea whose time had come.

"I'd say that every time one of those revolutionary regimes purged its artists it also killed itself a little bit," Bo interjected, putting down his fork.

"Possibly," Tok allowed, "but artistic creation isn't really a struggle with society but a struggle with yourself and with the great artists who came before you."

Soong admitted that one of the artists in the program Tina Dua would patronize was his mother. He would try to bring a cassette of her latest painting with him the next time he went home. Fesk was another painter whose work he found impressive. With a laser brush and Renaissance recalls, Fesk's enhancements made you feel that harmony was more than composition and beauty. Zeke told Soong he should call Tina over the weekend and asked if his mother had always been a painter.

"No, no, it's a recent discovery for her," Soong answered.

"Something to flesh out the last century of her life?" Tok asked politely.

"That, too, no doubt," Soong kept his reserve.

"Ah, to be a colonist and an artist and to be able to live long," Tok smiled.

Soong refused to be goaded. "Yes, can you imagine the results if Michelangelo and Matisse could have struggled with their creations for a century or two?"

Tok squinted in a wondrous pose. "Ah but they, too, if they lived today, would have to play bingo—or emigrate."

"You just said great art escapes its own time."

"That's our luck—not theirs."

"That's true," Soong conceded. "It's also our luck that we can synthesize Michelangelo and Matisse and see enhancements of what they would have created had they lived to be a hundred and sixty or two hundred, to project their masterpieces forward.''

Iyabo wanted to know more and the conversation drifted into technicalities. To Jammu, it was like the Cyclops speculations about a civilization so advanced that life was programmed and blood-and-flesh conscience no longer necessary. Why didn't they all join silicon consciousness and gain immortality like Michelangelo and Matisse? Why go on living if UICs could project your potential exponentially, and make an enhancement of what you would be in your fullest silicon glory? Maybe art was the only transcendence that modern people could possibly give themselves. With the laser pen you'd draw your most perfect picture and you'd punch in the sixteenth and the nineteenth centuries and stand back and see the synthesis of all past masters enhance your drawing. Then you'd demand the projection of your own potential lifted to the UIC's ultimate degree and stand back again before filing yourself away on a cassette.

But Jammu's mind drifted back to the question at hand, and back to the evening over tea three months ago when Soong had revealed that the colonies would propose gericide. For decades it seemed planetary systems had turned their minds away from the growing mushroom, Soong had said, and there was no doubt that the beehives would, if not welcome euthanasia, at least feel very much relieved. Jammu had listened without betraying any emotions, even when Soong had said, "You're an Asian." Their eyes had met above the tea cups and Jammu had answered that regionalism was another anach-

ronism he didn't indulge in. He had stopped
the young colonist there, because there were
things a chairman couldn't hear if he were to
retain planetary impartiality. But he had wondered if Soong meant that life was a little
cheaper in Asia.

It was long after Soong had left that Jammu
had found the answer to the terrible innuendo,
"You're an Asian." He had tried to exonerate
the colonist, imagining that Soong had only
meant a geographical description, that colonists
used such particulars in all innocence, and his
unwillingness to attribute geocentric malice to
Soong had led to illumination. It was almost
with shame that he realized it, but geriatric sanitation would not only help Asia, it would lower
the mushroom burden for everybody. It would
lower the social overhead whether you were a
drag-behind or a global standard system. He was
glad Tok had mentioned this before dinner. It
would indeed be naive not to realize that
euthanasia was in the systems' economic interest.

"Here you are, sir." Kapoor beamed at his elbow. "Fiber pudding with real whipped cream!"

The dessert *was* alluring.

Kapoor bent toward him. "Compliments of
our Bengali chef," he whispered with a glint in
his black eyes. "For you, sir."

Jammu smiled to himself and as Kapoor disappeared he thought of the prodigious human
variety of his own system. He dipped a teaspoon
into the dessert. Then, to his shocked amaze-
ment, he realized that none of the others had
whipped cream on their fiber pudding.

3

The moment Soong Ast got inside his office and saw Zad's face, he knew she hadn't reached anybody.

"No?" he asked.

Han, Viu and the two secretaries watched him. "And Hibs Koa?"

"They're paging him," Zad answered.

He almost wanted Zad to play back her phonecall. To see the communications room at the twin cylinders and to hear the person on duty would be reassuring.

The visiphone rang and Zad picked it up immediately. After a moment, she hung up. "The Koas are at a dinner party at the residence of Gab Fagbure."

"Who?"

"Fagbure, the UNCTAD adviser."

Bioethically, Soong wanted Han and the others to stay, but premordially he needed to be alone with Zad. He only had a minute.

Zad was punching Fagbure's name into the UN directory and a second later the screen spelled out his number.

But Soong shook his head. "That's all right."

He dismissed Han and the others and remained standing at Zad's desk, looking down into her oval face and trusting eyes.

"We tried," he said softly.

She was still eager. "I'm sure Hibs will come to the phone immediately when I say who's calling."

"We're starting the night session in a minute."

They looked at each other for a moment of silence and complicity.

"Can you stall things?" she asked.

"I'm sure I can hold the barrier till tomorrow. Why did he say that? He found the metaphor odd and inadequate.

Before dinner when he had dashed down here with his note and explained the situation to Zad and the others, she had started dialing the twin cylinders before he was even through explaining. She understood what he expected of her and he had watched her dial with gratitude. Colonists never felt more fulfilled, he realized, than when they put up with discomforts for the sake of principles; their separateness here, their alienness, might be their armor and their limits. She had understood why he had to join his colleagues upstairs. To recapitulate to her had made him realize that it was impossible to hold the barrier, that a consensus was synthesizing, that he would be outvoted. The night session was a maneuver against him, against gericide. The others wanted voluntary abstention. Why shouldn't *he*? Why shouldn't he, if the irritating detail of couples never getting around to procreating could be worked out?

Zad asked what she should say if the council returned her call while he was in session.

"Explain the dilemma but try not to sound alarming." He realized he was asking the impossible. "I mean, gericide is our position."

"Everybody knows that."

"I feel I can't abandon that position alone."

Zad's eyebrows rose in polite surprise. "But why can't you abandon gericide for something equally beneficial? You're fourth power, too."

They were waiting in the committeeroom, but he sat down on the edge of her desk and told her what he felt and what he meant. She listened, as she always did. Geriatric sanitation was something arrived at organically, and something half the planetary population felt was symbiotically logical and necessary. "Besides, nothing equally beneficial has really been proposed."

"Can't voluntary abstention be modifed so it'll work?"

"How?"

"I'm thinking." She bit her lip in a gesture of concentration and continued to play absentmindedly with the keyboard of her terminal.

Genetically, the two of them were as homogenized as anybody, he thought; metaphysically, too. The extra melting of the races in the colonies had produced a high frontier population of bronze-skinned people with autocratic features, broad noses like Zad's and wavy black hair like his, strong and handsome teeth and sensuous lips and, like Hibs Koa and Vui, narrow chins that gave some of them an expression of placid acuteness. Space had produced bright people, gifted individuals, but it gave them no experience in making solitary decisions. Individualism was an obsolete word among the stars, a short-lived romantic notion of nineteenth and twentieth century western prehistory. Colonies were closed-cycle systems in which there was neither leakage nor loss. Singularity was not possible.

He wished Zad's terminal would spring to life and that someone from the twin cylinders would fade in on the screen, but somehow he knew it wouldn't happen.

"I've got to get back," he said. He got up from the desk thinking of Tina Dua and mentally comparing her with Zad. It was unfair and it was dangerous, because it was contrary to the innate sense that he should find everything he needed in Zad.

"Would you like to come home with me for the weekend," he asked spontaneously. "It's my mother's birthday."

"But . . .?"

"I'd like you to meet her. You can change the reservation you made for me this morning to two." He could see his offer came as a surprise.

She looked at him and he felt she understood he was choosing her, that his invitation was something more than mundanity, even something more than a beginning of courtship.

"I'd love to," she said. Her smile was sufficiently out of office character to make him know she did understand.

"It's a deal," he winked. As he walked toward the exit he told himself that his choosing had something to do with evolution.

"It may be late," he said, turning at the door.

"I'll be here," she smiled.

"I appreciate that."

Feelings were treacherous and values were collective, not individual. The high frontier had a way of restraining private lives and of seeing things in terms of cost-benefits. It didn't have glamorous caprice. Zad was not Tina Dua. Her uniqueness was her magnificent reality, her vital safeguards.

4

Ter Ki put her handbag under her chair and looked up at the chairman before she sat down. Only the colonist and Iyabo Att were not back yet.

She should have phoned Mag to say she was doing overtime. But she hadn't trusted herself out there. She would blurt out something. She had seen the commotion in the hallway on the way back from the technopols' cafeteria. Reporters were going on the air right there, telling audiences the committee members were secluded even during the dinner recess. She had hurried past them, fearing someone might stop her and ask her things. "We have with us here Miss Ter Ki of the Hundred and Forty system, who tells us . . ." God, she'd rather die. She had seen two famous correspondents from her system.

Even in the half-empty cafeteria she hadn't trusted herself. With her tray, she had walked over to eat with Patel Nobu. The guard hadn't said much; only that the veal was the same they served the delegates tonight, that he had spent two years in a colony, that he was studying astrophysics at night school and couldn't wait to get out there again. On her mother's side, she had relatives on a torus. If she hadn't thought it unprofessional, she might almost have asked him if he had caught the howler Moscom had proposed. How could the delegates let it pass? If she had to wait until her grandmother died, she'd never have kids. She was quite sure of that.

No young women ever would, or almost, because they'd be old themselves before their parents passed away. She had seen the colonist take notes toward the end; maybe he would voice the logical objection, or try to amend the amendment to make it work.

Zeke Dua and Bo Lim were chatting, Dua sitting tilted back and with his feet on his desk. She liked him, maybe because of the furrows and lines that gave his young face character. Lim was insufficient, not so much because he did anything wrong, but because there wasn't much of him. He looked tired, too. Of course he had traveled the previous night.

She watched Patel tug his service weapon to the side with one hand and run the other hand through his crewcut as if to be sure he looked all right. She envied him. Tomorrow she'd be back with some dumb subcommittee while he would be hearing the rest of the story. Unless the dénouement came tonight. She was a little confused; the lines of confrontation shifted so often and she couldn't see the beginning of a symbiosis. She had liked Dua's plea for old age and the need to respect seniors. It was still like that in some parts of the Hundred Forty system. She wondered whether Dua had read *Narayama*. There were places where people had been so poor that they had to sacrifice their old people. The story was about an old premordial woman whose life had been good and whose son loved her very much. But when he married she decided it was time to go to Narayama, the mountain where old people were abandoned. A very sad story.

She turned on the master and looked up at the

chairman. Maybe she could ask to become the
Unisave secretary for the quarter. She knew of
chairmen requesting permanent assignments,
but that was of course for other reasons, *those*
kinds of reasons.

She wasn't sure she wanted to see Bo Lim's
proposal pass—that is, if it could be amended so
it would work. She didn't mind seniors, but
some of them were so old they didn't seem to
belong to the same world as the rest of them. Just
the other night at the Asean reception, Mag and
she had witnessed the painful antics of a pair of
antique diplomats. The two centenarians had
egged each other on and talked too noisily about
the good old days. The hostess had tried to stare
them down but they were too drunk and the
Singaporean chief of technopols had managed to
steer them out on the near-empty roof garden.
There, they were crying in each other's arms that
this was "the fuckingest of brave new worlds."
The guests had been uncomfortable. The old
men had shouted they were the only real people
there. "I'm a hundred and sixty-three," one of
them had yelled at the Singaporean. "I was
born in Boston when there was still a Yoo-nited
States and fertility was not a dirty word!" She
had been tempted to go out on the roof garden, to
hush them down and ask what had been so great
about their youth, when Mag had introduced her
to a polytech with gray eyes. The senior Bosto-
nian shouted Unisave was grappling with the
wrong questions, leading to false dilemmas. The
silly thing was that the polytech and she lost
each other in the commotion when the host finally escorted the two seniors to the door.

They all turned as Nobu opened the door and

let Iyabo in. Two camerapens on sticks tried to get in with her, but the two guards on the outside pushed the reporters back. Ter noticed Iyabo's headscarf was tied differently.

"Crazy," Iyabo sighed with a gesture toward the door. "One of them wanted me to confirm that the colonies will take any Unisave member who may lose at bingo."

Ter could see Dua knew this meant him.

"They sure don't waste time out there," Zeke said uncomfortably, moving his feet off his desk.

Iyabo crossed to her seat. "Oh, they don't know what to speculate."

"Guard!" Nagpur said.

Nobu sprang to attention.

"Are you sure nobody can bug the door or the wall?" the chairman asked, pointing to the length of the wall from the door to the water-cooler.

Nobu was quite sure this was not possible but if the chairman wanted him to, he'd ask his colleagues outside to clear the hallway fifteen meters back. Belem agreed. They should be sure no listening devices could be put against the wall.

"They don't know anything," Iyabo announced. "They also asked me if bingo winners could sell their winning tickets to losers."

"Somebody asked me if gericide will become law by midnight," Tok yawned.

"Why would anyone sell a winning ticket?" Belem wondered.

"Maybe if a spouse of a hundred years was a loser, you'd want to go together," Iyabo offered.

But the chairman nodded and Nobu opened the door and conferred with his colleagues outside. They turned to face the mediapeople and

Nobu closed the door and took up a martial position in front of it. Faintly, they all heard the howl of protest.

"All right, so where's Soong?" Tok asked.

"He said he had to go to his office for a second," Lim said.

Ter felt this was the moment to ask the chairman, but she knew she didn't have the courage. When she glanced up at him, he looked so intimidating that she decided he had problems enough. Maybe she could call his office and say she had worked the session the day Bo Lim proposed voluntary birth limitation and that she would like to work Unisave permanently. Her grandmother had told her that to ask was the cheapest thing on earth. Maybe in five minutes, she lied to herself.

Tok wondered aloud whether it had been such a good idea to clear the hallway. "Now they'll really speculate."

"So what?" Belem asked.

Ter saw the chairman wasn't listening but reading something. She felt relieved; she couldn't ask now.

"Aren't you scared of the media?" Tok asked the general.

"Why be afraid of them," Belem asked lazily. "They're not dangerous."

The chairman didn't react.

"Who's dangerous?" Tok asked.

"We are."

Ter thought the general was joking.

"The media aren't dangerous," Belem continued. "You can see that in war coverage; when one side is winning they write the news one way and when the winds of fortune change, they

report events the other way. They always strain
too hard to be on the right side of issues."

Ter looked up and saw Nagpur's eyes were
closed. The chairman had his hands under the
chin and his long, handsome fingers framed his
face to the temples. She realized that she wasn't
supposed to see this. He looked too private. His
hands both shielded and soothed his temples
and she had a feeling that he belonged to an
older world than the rest of them. He was like a
premordial statue. She wondered if this was how
you prayed. Her grandmother had told her that
to pray was to converse with people who are no
more. But the chairman's dilemma was people
who were and people who were not yet.

As she lowered her eyes, Nobu opened the
door and Soong Ast walked in. There was no
commotion outside. Of course not; the newspeople had been moved back fifteen meters.

"I'm sorry," the colonist apologized and hurried to his seat.

PART IV

1

Zeke Dua rasped his voice and leaned forward as the chairman said, "All right, Iyabo, gentlemen!" and the little secretary rolled the master.

"I would like the floor," Zeke said.

Jammu nodded and Zeke suggested that gericide and Lim's voluntary birth limitation be formally tied together. The colonist proposal sought to eliminate a third of all persons sixty and over and Lim suggested that voluntary abstention on an individual, family basis could spare the bingo losers altogether. "To that I added that persons wholly without descendants should be allowed to live completely outside the pall of euthanasia. I may just as well amend that to read: such childless persons shall be exempt from any form of population sanitation regardless of voluntary birth limitation."

He looked across at Soong. "That way the colonies won't have to take me if I lose in four years."

Soong looked blank and Iyabo leaned toward him and explained what it was that a reporter had asked her.

Zeke continued. "The question is therefore whether voluntary, do-it-yourself measures will make a big enough dent, something that shouldn't be too difficult to metapoll. As far as I can see, this evening's only two objectives are: one, to hammer out directives for statistical feedback to our Dynamics and Demographics subcommittees and, two, to decide what we tell the planet in the meantime. I personally think that if we stick to Lim's family planning, public response will be favorable."

Iyabo asked what, in his opinion, they should tell the planet in the meantime.

"The truth, or as close to the truth as we can manage," he answered, watching her across the horseshoe.

"It's dangerous to raise hopes," Belem said.

Zeke hunched his shoulders. "I don't know. People have known about gericide for six weeks now. If we say that young people choosing to delay having families may help solve the problem I can't see why that's so traumatic. Let's spend the next half hour on what Demographics should ask and the following hour to draw up a statement. We can be out of here by 2300." For effect he checked his digit.

"Promise?" Iyabo smiled, looking from Tok to him.

Before anyone could interrupt, Zeke asked if he could have a quick vote on the following draft request to Demographics. But as he began to formulate the directive, Tok gently asked how he—and Lim—envisaged enforcing the do-it-yourself grandma salvage program.

Lim explained. "I, a full quota husband, and my full quota wife refuse to wait until my grandfather dies, for example. If my grandfather is a bingo loser, he will then be eliminated. It's as simple as that."

Soong raised a hand and kept it in the air until he had everybody's attention. It didn't take long, Zeke noticed.

"Well, well," smiled Tok, leaning back in his chair. "The colonies want the floor."

With a nod to Nagpur, Soong said it was a mere point of order. He was sorry actually, he said, but as a gynecologist he couldn't see how any woman could postpone childbearing much beyond sixty-five, even with estrogen treatment and UIC monitoring during pregnancy. And a woman of sixty-five would have a ninety-five-year-old mother and father and her grandparents would be a mere hundred and twenty-five. Unless her parents and grandparents—not to talk about her in-laws—were wiped out by accident or catastrophic illness, it was unlikely that she would ever procreate. Or was there something he had missed here?

Soong looked from the chairman to Bo on his left.

Zeke noticed a kind of I-told-you-so smile on the secretary's face and damned himself for not having caught on earlier. Why hadn't anyone?

Soong turned toward Bo and repeated his question. "Did I miss something?"

Soong tried to be apologetic as he said to Bo that there was no reason why people of their generation couldn't live to be several hundred years old.

All eyes were on the Muscovite who, after a fleeting glance at Soong, didn't seem to know where to look. "I really don't know what to say," he mumbled, opening his folder.

Zeke felt the discomfort and the pain in the room. They all wanted to defeat the colonist's objections but no one could counter Soong's impeccable logic. Bo flipped through his folder with a trifling gesture as if he knew it couldn't possibly contain the answer. Zeke could feel each mind racing over the objection and each running into the same wall.

"Seems tit for tat family planning is more radical than we'd imagined," Tok said softly.

But Jammu Nagpur took things in his hands. As deftly as ever, he steered over the dead point, over Lim's embarrassment and Tok's soft attempt at sarcasm by going back to square one. Under debate, he said, was the colonist proposal to eliminate one third of all earthside persons sixty years of age or older. An amendment, offered by Bo Lim, introduced the notion of voluntarily delaying procreation on a family basis. The amendment had led to discussions of the right to live vs. the right to reproduce, which in turn had made Zeke Dua suggest that the principle of exempting parents of couples who voluntarily delay childbearing be extended to all persons without offspring.

"Maybe that's it," Sal interrupted with a sly grin.

Zeke swiveled to look at the big Brazilian next to him.

"Yes?" Jammu said, lengthening the suspense.

The general crossed his arms and grinned. "Before Soong shot down voluntary abstention, I was thinking that if a young man and wife refused to delay having a family until some parent kicks the bucket—and only one parent, Soong, not all of them, if we stay with the one-for-one rationale—they should maybe suffer the same fate themselves."

Sal looked around the horseshoe, then added,

"In other words, if you don't want to wait, you condemn yourself to live to be sixty only."

Zeke was tempted to say, Now you're talking! But his mind raced ahead, looking for a way to make it work.

"But that was *before*," Tok said soberly. "Also, that's an awful lot of generational responsibility up and down, although of course in premordial times, they had that too. . . ." He let his sentence dangle.

"How about combining the two," Sal wondered. "The longer you delay the longer your bingo-losing parent gets to live."

"You mean twenty years gained is twenty years," Zeke said, to keep the idea going.

"Better than that," Sal continued. "When it becomes your turn, as a parent who waited, to play bingo, you get twenty years added if you lose."

"Won't be pretty," Tok sighed. "Each generation with the knife at its predecessor's throat, everybody hostage to their kids. 'Come on sonny, give your mom another year.' "

But Belem wouldn't give up. Old people had always lived at the mercy of their descendants, in neolithic tribal societies or in modern systems. You paid your social security during your active years in the hope that the next generation would honor it. The whole thing reminded him of evac hovers during the war. The choppers could lift so-and-so many and you had to shoot off those who tried to hang on to the skids. The point here was the room they had to work with, the planetary load factor. A sexagenarian who lost in the crap game was superannuated the moment someone else was born. Their only room for maneuver was the time before someone else was born.

Zeke could imagine the shift from Moscom's family responsibility to the opposite—two UIC-generated planetary figures matched up every New Year's Day—22,070,556,792 minus 22,068,764,402. Bingo losers would live in the difference, a kind of demographic limbo. He thought of Nasiba Riss and his own idea last night to begin sanitation in the oldest end of the over-sixty spectrum. Maybe *they* should live in the year-to-year limbo. The only trouble was of course that there were so few, relatively speaking, on the top of the age pyramid. The annual sanitation would look disproportionately horrifying. To sanitize a third of all sexagenarians would be a deep cut in the fattest part of the demographic bulge; to eliminate all those who had lived longest would be chopping off the whole top of the pyramid. They were back to justice—like six weeks ago.

He watched Bo and wondered why he had proposed a solution that was unworkable. Bo was a bioengineer, not a demographer. Was Moscow *protecting* Misha Sev by having a young innocent propose something that could only be a stalling operation. Was there a second act to this? Would Misha be back next week with the real solution?

He felt sympathy toward Lim. He vaguely knew Lo Hals, a remarkable scientist who apparently had been Bo's boss. Was the solution in bioengineering? Was there some biochemical way of keeping bingo losers outside the realm of demography?

Sal and Tok talked about the room for maneuver and Zeke told himself that if the way to defeat geriatric sanitation was to chisel, they sure were chiseling, even with military metaphors. But the planet was waiting. After dinner he had called his office, and Bi Flan had been all feverish excitement. All sorts of people had called, "from Hoo down to your wife." Flan had apologized as soon as he realized his gaffe and Lan had come on the screen, cool and collected, to convey Washington's anxiety. Why were they going into night session? He had resisted her, but with a few hmms and ah-has had managed to confirm that they were perhaps up to something. The networks had carried his impromptu interview, she said, and commentators were now interpreting his "life is priceless as long as you can be compassionate about others" to mean a consensus was emerging. "But that was this morning," he had cautioned. She had looked so disappointed he had told her they should all go home, but she had insisted no one was even thinking of leaving until he came out of the session. "We'll watch a movie between bulletins from your end of the corridor," she had snipped. He had resisted her bait but said she could meet him at the committeeroom as soon as she heard they were coming out. To let her go on video with him was another way of placating her.

He leaned forward. In the meantime, the seven of them would have to diffuse the expectations this burning of midnight oil was provoking. He could understand why Tok and some of the others were eager to come to grips with the question that kept the planet on tenterhooks, but

Jammu and he had been right in voting against
a night session. Now they would have to come
up with some third act resolution that would
satisfy people's need for a discharge of pent-up
anticipation. His hopes had been with the do-it-
yourself family planning. Now, he couldn't see
how they could get around Soong's logic.

Something in his experience told him they
should fall back on the true and the tried. The
first thing to diffuse was their own emotions,
their own discouragement. They were not here
to understand the inevitable, he had said this
morning, but to challenge it.

2

Had he been set up?

Bo's humiliated mind ran over the events of
the last seventy-two hours. The more he thought
it over, the more questions welled up inside him,
questions begging other questions. The most
mortifying question was why he hadn't spotted
the flaw himself—not last Sunday when they
had whisked him from his lab to the presidium
and told him, not Monday and Tuesday during
Lo Hals' briefing, not at the ceremony Wednes-
day morning. Even Hals' regard for Misha Sev's
sensitivity in telling him not to mention voluntary abstention to her seemed suspect. His own
vanity too, in not telling Dra any details. "You'll
be coming over next Tuesday," he had told her.
It was silly. He had been so supercilious, so

willing to play along with Hals and the others
and agree that for maximum effect the proposal
should be under wraps until he announced it in
Unisave. They hadn't told him he couldn't tell
his wife. It was his own inflated pride. Now, he
felt sure she would have seen through it.

Or was he imagining things? No one here had
caught on—except Soong that is. Why hadn't
Iyabo? Because she, like himself, was used to
thinking about life in terms of molecular chemis-
try? Again, his mind recapped the colonist's objections. They were airtight. Why hadn't anyone
in Moscow come up with them. Lo Hals' briefing
team had included a physician, he now remembered.

Or was Lo testing his intelligence in some
subtle way? Impossible. He was now a fourth
power person, installed with planetwide fan-
fare, and not easily called on the carpet by
technopols of his home system. Fourth power
status implied the highest osmosis, the highest
degree of synectics. Sal Belem had defined the
time frame they had for maneuvering. The obstacle had to be isolated, discerned, synergized
and obliterated. Ultraintelligence had estab-
lished that senility was not the bane of aging but
was caused by disease. If Soong said there was
no reason why their generation couldn't live for
several hundred years, why couldn't female re-
productive organs remain active for the same
time frame? Misha said the achievements of
computer intelligence in medicine were sensational, so why not?

He looked at his manila folder and suppressed
an urge to hurl it across the room. He knew the
amendment by heart and there was nothing in it

about women getting too old for childbearing while waiting for their next-of-kin to die off. If only his mind could expand exponentially. If only the seven of them could achieve true synectics.

Soong was speaking. The point, said the colonist, was that humanity had developed a long-range view of the evolution of intelligence.

"Exactly," Tok said, throwing himself back in his chair with impatience. "This whole idea of limits to growth, limits to people should be repulsive to you."

"But it is," Soong shot back.

"It should be totally alien to the thrust and awareness that you stand for."

Soong nodded but Tok wasn't to be stopped. "In a year you're setting out for Alpha Centauri. The history outward is continuing. The colonies are the first stepping stones in the leap toward the stars. You're the best of all of us, the best in all of us."

"The mushroom is a planetary problem," Soong said patiently.

"In the short term, yes." Tok's voice was dramatic. "In the long-range view of things we're still the same species, Soong. People living to be a thousand will affect you, too, and not just because they'll force you to build more tin cans. You know the consequences are more subtle than that!"

"We can only call them as we see them. Now it's longevity vs. biomass. In ten years it may be that the structural development of human intelligence isn't conducive to deep space probing."

Tok grinned. "You mean we'll go a little funny in the head up there in the starships."

"Only the youngest members will be alive at the arrival."

Bo noticed that the guard at the door was looking up and listening.

"The voyagers will be on their own," Soong added.

But Zeke cut in before Tok could answer and asked Jammu if Demographics couldn't be directed to take metapolls on some of the aspects of the question they were grappling with. A direct input. Would *you* forego mother and/or fatherhood if by doing so you directly saved your father/mother from sanitation?

At the door, the guard returned to his reading and Bo also felt a letdown. He would have liked to hear more. Dra's brother said everybody in the Cyclops program was betting that there were no more tensions between the limbic system and the cerebral cortex in extraterrestrial brains, that a lasting peace among brain components might be a precondition for long-lived civilizations.

But Zeke had the floor and said he wanted a quick overnight Arbitron to give them an idea of the dimensions they were looking for as well as some indication of the limits they were up against. Bo thought of his former boss. In the ground car taking them to the presidium, Lo Hals had said they could have found no better replacement for Misha Sev. "I'm more comfortable with cell synthesis than with roundtable synthesis," he had objected, looking from Lo to Dra in the back seat. "You're the best man, precisely because you know about recombinant methodology," Lo had grinned. Right now he failed to see the connection—or the joke.

Zeke was finishing. "Of course I want the

overnight poll to be direct and universal."

Zeke was interrupted by Iyabo. "Shouldn't the Arbitron be directed at quotapersons only?"

"Why?" Zeke asked with a tired smile.

"Obviously, women over childbearing age will say yes to renouncing motherhood."

"Guess you've got a point there," Zeke conceded.

Bo wondered why Zeke had tried to stack the odds. Was the world more devious than imagined? He hated to be unsuspecting.

The chairman suggested only quotapersons be polled. "I realize the pros may be somewhat lower," Jammu said, looking at Zeke, "but such a poll will be more convincing."

"Please believe me," Zeke huffed. "I wasn't trying to start anything."

Jammu leaned forward with a silent frown. "We're looking for consensus, not a new skirmish on the age front."

Zeke found his composure again. "I'm sure they can program the right mix."

Jammu gaveled lightly and asked for a vote on Zeke Dua's proposal to direct the subcommittees to take samples for metadetermination "in various demographic mixes of growth, density and age profiles."

The hands of Zeke, Iyabo and Tok shot up. Belem's hand followed, joined by the chairman's own hand.

"I abstain," Soong said.

"Against?" the chairman asked.

Bo raised his hand. He was still confused and voting against something made him feel a little better.

3

Sal Belem looked across at Iyabo and Soong as Zeke next to him finished polishing the language of the poll they had just voted on. Finally they were getting somewhere.

Jammu suggested they have the legal people finetune the wording, but Iyabo interrupted to say that if only quotapersons were polled, you should limit the sampling to people with living parents. "To be fair to Zeke," she smiled.

It reminded Sal of the unused quota debate three years ago. What happens when a couple with one child divorces, that is, a couple with one unused quota? He had been in favor of giving the unused quota to the wife—for purely practical reasons since only she possessed a womb, but Ken Wei and Jammu had been in favor of the father. Tok had wondered aloud if the colonies and Asian societies were patriarchal and they had started the old argument of which came first, the chicken or the egg. Jammu had argued that the carrier of the sperm had the right of initiative. The point was subtle. It was then that the idea of a lottery had cropped up the first time. In the interest of Solomonian justice, each divorcing couple with a spare quota should play heads and tails. Sometimes the husband would win; sometimes the wife—demographically it didn't matter. In the end they had decided to leave it up to the local Population

Care boards—their "hour of cowardice," Tok had jeered. The point was remote. Actually, it was only when the partners of a dissolved marriage with one child *both* remarried other divorcees who had fulfilled their two quotas that the spare surplus quota came into play.

Sal sneaked a peek at his digit. It was 2205. If he was optimistic, he agreed they might be out of here in another hour. But it was hard to look at the bright side of things right now.

He became aware of Iyabo looking at Tok next to him and followed her glance. Sort was putting his metal wastepaper basket on the desk in front of him. It was grotesque, the gray metal container on the desk. It was so tall Tok was almost hidden by it.

Sal let his glance wander. To his right, Zeke was talking poll language and Jammu taking notes, but the little secretary was watching Tok. Bo Lim was also looking.

Tok was always terribly superior and conceited and, when impatient, given to silly outbursts, but Sal had never seen him put a wastepaper basket on his desk before. During the week of the gericide debate, Tok had called for the sanitation of the planet's remaining believers and suggested such mercykillings would make believers live up to their faiths since most premordial religions maintained a bonus for martyrs. When Misha had objected that believers would forswear their gods, Tok said they would be apostates and promised eternal hellfire. "Without disrespect for the colonist proposal, I think mine will solve the question with even more fairness since only the Just go to heaven and we will rid the planet of its most backward population." You never knew when to laugh at Sort's sallies.

Sal looked with increasing curiosity as Tok pulled a marker from his uniform breastpocket. Zeke was telling Jammu that econometrics *could* be a factor, but nobody paid attention except the chairman. They all watched Tok as he began marking sheets of his scratch pad, carefully shielding his handwriting behind the waste basket. With a self-absorbed smile, Tok folded his scratch pad sheets.

Zeke admitted that *some* references to gericide would have to be in the language.

Sal wondered if Tok was making origami flowers or paper airplanes.

The chairman looked up. Zeke became aware of the direction of Jammu's glance and swiveled around to see what only he had missed.

"What the hell are you doing?" Zeke asked testily.

Tok kept smiling and Nagpur's face contracted into a quizzical frown.

"Making ballots," Tok answered.

"Oh not tonight," Zeke groaned dramatically. "Whatever you think we are, Tok. No games. Please!"

Tok continued folding his scratch pad ballots. With a weary sigh Zeke returned to his poll language, saying he would be through in one minute. Tok put his ballots into his waste basket. Knowing all eyes were on him, he got up, looked from face to face and put both hands on the waste container.

"You make me nervous!" Zeke said.

Tok remained standing, a trace of a smile on his handsome face.

"Okay, I'm through," Zeke huffed, throwing himself back in his chair.

With theatrical suspense, Tok lifted his waste basket and shook it.

"Guard please!" he said suddenly without turning around.

Nobu got up from his chair, looking bewildered.

"May I borrow your laser, please!" Tok said, putting down his waste basket.

Nobu felt his holster with a dumb expression as if to be sure the weapon was there. Then he looked to the chairman for support.

"Your laser, please," Tok repeated without turning to face the security guard.

"Tok?" Iyabo asked with a trace of anxiety in her voice.

Tok didn't look across at her but stood leaning on his container with a boyish grin. "All right then," he said, "will you just hand your laser to the chairman."

"Sir?"

Sal knew how underlings could stubbornly make the system work for them.

"I said just hand your laser to the chairman!" Tok said.

Sal swiveled around and watched the guard, who seemed to be trying to remember what to do in a situation like this, a situation that probably wasn't in his instruction manual anyway. Brusquely, Nagpur gestured to the guard to execute Sort's bizarre wish.

The man took his time and Sal savored every moment of it.

Nobu unhooked the laser, crossed with deliberate slowness behind Sal and Zeke to the

chairman's desk. Sal swiveled with him. At
Jamu's desk, Nobu just stood there holding the
weapon in his hand until Nagpur told him to put
it down. The laser was heavy and to Sal the thud
sounded real.

"Just hold it, Jammu," Tok said gently.

The chairman eyed the weapon in front of him
with suspicious eyes.

"If you're trying for melodrama you've made
your point," Zeke snapped at Tok.

"Just hold it, Jammu," Tok repeated patiently.

With a grimace of aversion, Nagpur picked up
the laser. It was heavier than he had expected.
Sal was sure it was a .9 millimeter. They had had
lasers like this, slightly older models, after
Alegre.

"I thought we've been pretty abstract about
life," Tok smiled as Nagpur balanced the laser
on its handle, carefully keeping his finger away
from the trigger. Sal could feel the tension in the
room and the old gush of adrenal juices in his
own body. Across from him the colonist sat
stonefaced, his eyes darting between Tok and his
absurd waste basket and the chairman with the
laser.

"Always ends, not the means," Tok continued
while he shuffled his ballots in his waste basket.
"Our good Jammu now holds the means. Maybe
we should try a game of colonist roulette ourselves."

Sal loved it. The laser in the chairman's
hand—his amateur hand—and Tok's calculating
playfulness made everything come alive. Sal
pushed his chair back so he could take in the
whole scene. The Muscovite narrowed his eyes
and tried not to look bewildered.

Carefully, Jammu put down the laser, with the barrel pointing out over the secretary's head and the horseshoe toward the wall between Tok and Bo Lim. The guard remained standing beside the chairman, as if he had decided it was more important to remain close to the weapon than to the door.

"Suppose we start sanitizing that one-ninth of all of us we find so intolerable," Tok began.

"Jammu," Zeke interrupted. "May I formally ask you to put an end to this!"

Iyabo broke out in a forced laugh. "Why do you object to Eurocom's proposal for exclusive bingo for Unisave members, Zeke?"

"Not Eurocom, Iyabo," Tok smiled across at her. "I challenge you to continue the search for osmosis on a more intimate scale. Only one of us will have to die."

Sal watched. Jammu obviously was going to let Tok go through with his little divertimento. Tok stood leaning on his waste basket, defiant and provocative. Soong seemed to be calculating—distance or time? Sal wondered—while Bo kept his eyes on the laser in a stare that was alarming and faintly comic. Iyabo was fidgeting with her zigzag armband and her smile was frozen. Sal looked up at the chairman. There was something masklike, emotion-purged in Jammu's face that he had never seen before.

"We're here in the name of a plurality . . ." Zeke started in an even voice, but Tok interrupted him with sudden anger.

"Forget the rest of humanity," Tok said sharply. "That's the point of this little exercise."

Zeke and Tok looked at each other past Sal.

With a forbidding face, Zeke got up. Sal
sprawled back in his chair, between the two
standing men, and he felt the tension. Tok kept
his arm on his incongruous waste basket and
stared back at Zeke.

Sal heard Iyabo's anxious voice say, "Zeke?
Tok?" but he kept his eyes on Zeke towering
over him and holding Tok's gaze.

The moment Zeke stepped back from his desk
and turned, Sal knew the chairman's tactical
error was not having the door covered by the
guard. Zeke walked slowly, deliberately.

They all heard the scrape as Jammu picked up
the laser. Zeke swung around. He was maybe
three steps from the door.

"I dare you to play bingo," Tok said.

The remark was superfluous, gratuitous. Sal
tilted himself up a little so he could see Jammu.

Zeke kept his eyes and his dignity on Jammu
and on the laser pointed at him.

Sal realized that if he hadn't stretched himself
low like that, he would have been in the line of
fire.

4

Zeke could tear the door open before Jammu
even found out how to blast him. There were
guards on the other side of the door and the
reporters were fifteen meters down the hall.
Thoughts cascaded into the center of his
mind—the memory of the only time a patient

had gone into arrest, the oscilloscope beep coming faster and faster and the anesthesiologist jabbing a syringe of lidocaine into the IV line. Thirty seconds and the world wouldn't be the same again. He knew that was why the chairman was holding him at laserpoint.

He felt his adrenals pushing up his heart rate. He took a deep breath and told himself that what made him stay was curiosity, plain old what-happens-next curiosity. The glow of Jammu's pitch-black eyes held his own gaze in a hypnotic vise, and the room was so silent that by the door he thought he could hear the small talk down the hall. It had been eighteen years ago, but he could still see himself with the needle holder in his right hand and a pair of fine-toothed forceps in his left hand. "Holy shit, the guy's going to arrest," Dr. Ruz had yelled. It was his only operating room death.

Slowly, Jammu lowered the laser, and a second later Sal Belem shot up in his chair.

"Please sit down—both of you," Jammu said in his ordinary voice.

Zeke remained standing. It was all crazy, like the operating room, reaching for a penlight and seeing the black area almost filling the clear cornea. The idea of calling Soong's bluff on gericide didn't displease him but he hated Tok's smug theatricals.

"Please." The chairman's voice was commanding as if he was impatient with fools.

Tok sat down and ceremoniously lifted his waste basket to the right between himself and Bo, who looked pale and embarrassed. Jammu put down the laser with the barrel again pointing over the head of the little secretary. The guard stood next to the chairman like his avenging angel.

"Zeke," Iyabo said softly.

He felt silly. The sting of age again. Jammu and he should be the wisest since they were the oldest, but all he felt was a sense of ridicule. His own huff was foolish. They were all tired, overwrought. He expected Jammu to apologize but the chairman asked each of them to go into himself.

"Let us be ourselves, in all humility," Jammu said.

Zeke just stood there, three steps from the door. If he remained defiant long enough, Jammu would have to play for his sympathy.

"Of all the follies of men our own are usually the worst," Jammu said. "All we can do is show each other the alternatives truthfully and lovingly."

Zeke watched the chairman and sensed that Jammu knew he was out on unfamiliar waters, but that he was struggling back toward sanity. Curiosity again—and the sense of his own absurdity standing there—made him relent and walk back to his seat.

Jammu spoke. "We have all had sleepless nights, I'm sure, all agonized over the question crushing us. We have never committed murder, perhaps we won't have to. Perhaps Bo Lim's amendment is the solution—it looked that way earlier. I ardently hope so. Man shouldn't soar to the stars on a rainbow of cadavers."

The chairman looked for a moment at Soong. Zeke felt the glance was almost fatherly.

"I feel almost elated," Jammu continued. "We must explore new territory—ourselves. If we

confront the true alternatives we may find all the
hidden energies within ourselves. We are differ-
rent in talents and intelligence, but I think we
can understand the experience of universal man
if we can understand each person's individuality. Zen texts say that the agony which comes
just before illumination provokes laughter. I am
tired of rectitude."

Zeke thought of that OR death eighteen years
ago. The man was in for a meniscectomy of the
right knee and he had removed the damaged
cartilage when the crisis came. The resident was
starting to cast the leg and Ruz aerating the patient when back-to-back runs of premature heart
contractions began and the beeping came faster
and faster. Diffuse cerebral edema had been the
primary diagnosis. He hadn't known then, but it
had been his last year at Fosters. In 2170 he was
appointed to the Bree commission, and the next
year Tina graduated.

He listened to Jammu say that if their goal was
humanity's salvation, as the acronym of their
committee said it was, they would have to be
human themselves. "We must explore the unsuspected," the chairman continued, "we must
penetrate the subversive, the dangerous within
ourselves. Our imaginations must seek the many
possible futures."

Jammu looked from face to face, then lowered
his eyes to the laser. His face was expressionless.
He didn't know what Tok had in mind, he continued, but this moment offered a chance. The
answers were no doubt buried within themselves. They should take advantage of the
perspective the laser afforded to look more

closely into the fearful symmetry they were confronting.

He added, "I believe the only force that can save us from self-destruction is reason and perhaps the ability to recognize the folly of most of the ideas we believe in. Sometimes the most important element of progress is the courage to stand still."

Jammu looked around the horseshoe from Sal to Iyabo and let his gaze come to rest on Tok. No, he didn't know what Tok wanted to prove with his waste basket and seven ballots, but . . .

"Nine ballots, Jammu," Tok interrupted gently. "We're nine in here."

Zeke looked at the secretary and the guard. The two technopols became self-conscious as they realized that all eyes were on them. They were like last-year med students on their first surgical rotation. The girl looked down on her monitors and Nobu produced a half-smile and a jerk of the head. They also reminded Zeke of the students two nights ago. During the question-and-answer period, one of them, quite lovely, had asked him to recall the greatest day in his life. He had passed over love, diplomacy and appointment to the Bree commission and told about the first operation he had performed. A bearded student had asked if Unisave didn't agree that mating had become demeaned since it was devoid of procreative transcendence—that is, except those two times a woman decapsulated.

"Kant maintains that every human being is an end in himself," Tok said with a smile. "That's what I like about Zeke's idea that no one has to

earn his right to exist. I'm sure there can be no
philosophical objection to our faithful guard and
charming secretary joining the human race."

Zeke thought the guard had both the candor
and the cool of the young. He also had some of
Soong's aloofness. The girl didn't have the looks
that made derestricted men turn and do doubletakes, but she had pretty eyes, a mixture of
brown and grey with flecks of black that had to
be pretty in dim light.

Tok continued "We're after the elusive nine-
point-something that has to go. If you'll forgive
the 'point-something . . .' After all, with the
laser we can't imitate Shylock and deal in fractions of flesh."

Zeke was about to say you'd be surprised what
you can do with fractions of anatomy.

"But you were saying, Jammu?" Tok stopped
eloquently.

"The fearful symmetry."

Zeke felt the chairman had seen through Tok's
game and was warning him.

Jammu didn't take his eyes from Tok as he
continued. "To look closely into the relation of
one happening to the other. Our task is the
paradoxical one of realizing our individuality
and at the same time transcending it."

Zeke couldn't think of illumination; only of
the scandal awaiting them. Reality didn't stop
for illumination. In a short time they'd have to
get out of here. In the hallway, a hundred
camerapens awaited them, and behind the elec-
tronics the General Assembly, their home systems and twenty-two billion people. He hadn't
planned to end it all like this. It would hurt—
Tina more than himself maybe. She wouldn't

have tables at the ten best restaurants in town, she wouldn't host the right parties and snub the Hoos in Washington. She wouldn't cast Broadway revivals with Aly Fem. Tonight, she'd look at him in that way of hers. "And you just sat there?" she'd ask. He could see her accusing taunt and the wallscreen behind her with a newscaster recapping the sensational news one more time before cutting to the UN reporter holding his audiopen up to the guard. What could he do? However deeply they explored their inner selves, once they came down from their spiritual high, they'd tell everything— eventually. That, too, was human.

Jammu said Rani Mazure had been the first to realize the awesome symmetry. "Rani said the wonder of science is that it makes us understand the riddle of life. The puzzle of human nature, she said, is the riddle of the sphynx. It is the enigma whose purpose is to disturb us, to make us move forward."

Zeke's memory of Rani was her pre-homogenized blue eyes. They had attended her funeral—the chairman, Sal, Tok, Misha, Ken Wei, Iyabo, and himself. Tina had been with him and had said she hated those ancient rites, sprinkling of water, burning of incense. He could still smell the sickening sweet odor. Rani had believed in science. Last night, Twer had disparaged science, but what else was there? Without ruthless technology, without ultraintelligence, we would all sink into a Breughelian nightmare. Without high-tech agriculture, "untouched by human hands," civilization would come to a stop at a magnificent high noon before collapsing into a new Dark Age. Unido's clas-

sified doomsday scenario painted a gruesome
picture of agroregions invaded by starving
hordes, creating territories around new warlords
and slaughtering each other for the last protein.
What would happen to the old and the frail in
such a circumstance. He didn't remember if the
Unido scenario even dealt with the aged, but it
was not difficult to imagine that they would be
trampled down first. This morning, he had
talked about the noble role reserved for tomorrow's aged, the rich life that medical triumphs
made available for nearly everybody. History
had always heaped tremendous responsibilities
on old men. He should have told the Secretary of
State that the premordial American governments Hoo and he sentimentalized so much had
never managed to make progress coincide with
their political beliefs.

Unido had forwarded the doomsday scenario
at Jammu's request when they had debated
Malthus' Dismal Theorem. Ken Wei had read
The Essay on the Principle of Population into
the record. Since population tends to press to the
limit of available subsistence, since the power of
production is weaker than the power of reproduction and since the balance between population and resources can only be maintained by
various checks—all of which are kinds of either
vice or misery—population will always grow
until there is enough misery or enough vice, or,
more likely, a mix of both to achieve equilibrium. They had discussed the twentieth century
addendum that resources could be stretched if
slow income growth depressed demands. Misha
had pointed to the twenty-first century discovery that increased food invited population

growth and claimed there was a kind of law of development where, ultimately, every advance in high-tech agriculture and industrial science—not to talk about medical technology—had its equivalent harmful effect. Maybe longevity was part of Thomas Malthus' miseries and vices.

Jammu was still talking, still smoothing and pacifying and clawing back from the edge. But the psychodrama wasn't over. What was Tok going to do with the loser of his waste basket lottery? Tok was a marvelously verbal person and he had a way of letting words carry him too far. Zeke tried to remember how many quotas Malthus had had himself. Five or six. The reverend had disapproved of the use of prophylactics made of swine intestines and thought "moral restraint" should be suggested to couples on their wedding day.

This afternoon, he had skipped the examples of society's indifference and cruelty toward its seniors. They had drafted several situation papers at Berkeley. Many peoples had respected their elders as long as they were lucid and vigorous, but practiced euthanasia when they became decrepit and doddering. Siberian Eskimos easily persuaded old men and women who had become a burden to commit suicide. Sometimes they gave a party for an old man; seal meat was served and vodka flowed. His folk danced and sang and a son or a younger brother slid behind the old man and strangled him with a seal bone. The Hopis and the Crees in North America and the Boshimen in the Southcone were in the habit of taking decrepit elders to a specially-built hut away from the village, supplying them with a little water and food and abandoning them there. Ovid and Seneca showed old men both as sages and as lechers and buffoons. In *Plutus*, the old men gathering to decide the fate of the republic could barely walk. Latin poets in particular denounced the hideousness of old women. Horace said of Canidia, "your tooth is black, antique age furrows your forehead and your breasts are flappy like those of a mare."

He had noted one passage about early twentieth century Greenland Eskimos, who customarily committed suicide when they realized they were becoming a burden to their kin. Old men crawled into their kayaks, pushed the sealskin boat from shore and paddled away never to be seen again. There was the incident that Emile Victor had witnessed, an old cripple who couldn't sail away and asked his children to throw him into the icy sea. The man's children did as he said, but his clothes kept him floating. One of the daughters who loved him very much, Victor wrote, shouted to him: "Father, put the head under; the voyage will be shorter that way."

He had wanted to finish with that quote echoing in everybody's conscience, but he had been distracted by Soong's objection that the individual can't both claim he doesn't owe society anything and demand that society owes him an enriching old age. Not all premordial people sanitized their elders. Explorers to the Tierra del Fuego described the Yahgans' way of treating their aged with respect and said they found old widows running families with authority. Missionaries reaching the Arandas in northern Australia found a veritable gerontocracy just as the

Zandes in Sudan were discovered to be governed by old men. In traditional China, women were able to find in old age a refuge from the harshness of adulthood. But the situation papers showed the majority of mankind had always welcomed old age with sadness or revolt or, at best, with a kind of vital pessimism. He had skipped the subject because they were modern people and because progress was, by definition, putting one foot in front of the other, one building block on top of the other. Science usually discovered more than it was looking for and the seven of them had better catch their future like that, too, in the net of what they weren't looking for.

Jammu wondered aloud if people's craving for possessions and abundance was not the other side of the coin of a profound urge to endure. Zeke thought that his own urge to endure was nothing more than curiosity, a burning need to know what would happen next, to be alive to see tomorrow's video scanlines, to see the next century, even if in the longest view this was all ludicrous. The Milky Way was nothing more than shrapnel created by the big bang and they were sitting on one of the orbiting grains of planets of one of the hundreds of billions of stars of the galaxy. In the shorter view, Unisave would survive because the idea of Unisave was essential.

5

Sal Belem calculated distance in ceiling panels while the chairman asked for introspection. Four meters at the most. But he had to get around Zeke. If he pushed his chair back nonchalantly, as if to stretch, so as to be further back than Zeke, he would have less of a curve. If he swung his chair slightly to the right and braced his left leg against it, his takeoff would be even faster. The laser was on his side of the chairman's desk. But so was the guard.

"We have learned that we can't understand the single element unless we see it as part of a magnificent whole," Jammu said, adding that there was an element of subjectivity in all our perceptions. Since we are the instrument of our own knowledge—at least until UICs begin programming themselves—it should follow that we would want to repress all other desires for the sake of the desire to know. Yet we are never free from the tyranny of prejudice or from the distortions due to a narrow view.

Sal watched the guard with new curiosity. Young and therefore fast, but facing a situation he had never experienced. Jammu said that to procreate was also to play roulette. If he had remained a bachelor, it was also because he had never had the nerve for fatherhood. Adopt children, yes, taking care of life already here, yes; but being responsible for creating life when there was so much of it, no.

Sal told himself that the only question was whether the safety catch was on the right as on the models he had used. Jammu had held the laser with the awesome reticence of someone who had never handled a weapon before, and Sal had seen that the safety catch was in lock position. Jammu's pointing the thing at Zeke had been pure bluff. If he grabbed it in one leaping flash, he'd have to unlock the catch. Otherwise the guard would know. You never pulled the same stunt twice on the same audience.

Love, beauty, knowledge and the joy of life, Jammu said, retained their luster however wide our range of vision. Mediocre minds were subdued by misfortune, but great minds rose above it.

"I can only hope God is with us," Jammu said.

"Isn't divine intercession another crutch we must leave behind?" Tok asked the chairman.

Five leaps and they'd have a new situation. Ecoengineers dealt with movement in terms of potential concentration instead of actual mass. Metaprogrammers dealt with similarities, had their UICs look for overlaps and count associations that were mutually beneficial. But military commanders had ancient instincts and took the totally unexpected into account. On the eve of that October morning in 331 B.C., Alexander had stood his men in such a way that Darius' Persian armies had to fight into the blinding sun the next morning. Patton had said there were probably as many ways of winning a war as there were of skinning a cat. An ancient art had died with homogenization.

Bo spoke for the first time since Tok had put his waste basket on his desk, saying that he didn't care much whether a theoretical divinity existed. If anything, their predicament should make them test their own intelligence. He couldn't explain how his amendment had missed the point that women would age while waiting for their parents' demise. He would refer back to his ecosystem for clarifications. But that was in the future. Right now he only wanted them to concentrate on the hope his proposal seemed to contain. A while ago they had been close to a solution and even now he wouldn't be surprised if they were at the threshold of final population stability.

"We're always on the eve of something wondrous," Jammu said with irony in his voice, "always one last obstacle, one last battle and then paradise."

"Be reasonable, Jammu," Zeke said unexpectedly.

It was the curve around Zeke's seat that bothered Sal. And he couldn't lunge from the halfway mark since the chairman's desk was elevated and the guard was standing above it.

"Knowledge should make us recognize the things that have value on their own account," the chairman said.

Sal leaned back and rechecked the distance in ceiling panels. Thirty centimeters each; thirty, sixty, ninety. Four times. A leap per meter; five long strides. He listened to Jammu and remembered the only really religious person he had ever met. It had been strange, the man on his praying mat next to the ground car stand at Rabat's skyport. He had almost stumbled over the ragged figure lying face down on a mat and praying to an ancient prophet. In combat, men who clung to premordial religions died better than men who didn't believe in anything. That had been his experience, but they all died anyway. That, too, was the point.

"If we lose our sense of sympathy for any human life, we're lost," the chairman said.

"Face it, Jammu," Tok smiled. "God is dead, Mazure is dead and we're not looking too hot ourselves right now."

There was an edge in the chairman's voice as he asked Tok whether he actually believed the Golden Age was around the corner of just one last bloodbath. In the long view, sure, Tok answered. The Renaissance came after the black plague had killed a fourth of Europe's population. And hadn't all nation-states gloried in the feats of arms of their founding fathers. Now it was the remoteness of fourth power consequences that was awesome, the consequences of the action the seven of them were taking tonight.

Suddenly Iyabo spoke. "I wish Tok would go ahead with his little psychodrama. This debate is getting pointless."

But the chairman wondered whether discoveries were always ultimately beneficial. "We have come to accept the idea that the universe is filled with intelligent life and that our learning about it and sharing in its goals is our first step toward maturity. But the first contact eludes us. How far and how hard will we have to look?"

"When we make the first contact," Bo said, "we will know one great truth: that it is possible for a civilization to maintain itself."

"And not destroy itself?" Tok smiled.

Jammu said he leaned toward the depressing view that only by the sheerest accident would intelligent beings, if they existed, resemble us, even in intelligence. Bo quoted his brother-in-law as saying that first contact might tell us something about another intelligent species and that in turn might tell us what we most need to know about our own.

They were forgetting the laser, Sal realized.

"Isn't it all hopeless?" Jammu sighed. "The sun is dying."

"Not exactly tomorrow, Mr. Chairman," Tok answered.

"And there are trillions of other suns," Bo said.

"A couple of centuries ago people only knew how the universe started; now we know how it'll end."

"By singularity."

But Bo smiled. "If only we become smart enough."

"Excuse me," the guard said. "But isn't there a solution in space?"

They all looked at the youth. Their silence visibly intimidated him. He stood awkwardly next to the chairman, already regretting his audacity, almost looking for help from Soong Ast.

The chairman swiveled toward the guard and kindly asked, "What solution?"

6

Standing next to the chairman, Patel Nobu told them that the stars were made of plasma.

He wished he could speak like Professor Las. Until nuclear physics, man was concerned with the three states in which matter was commonly found. Yet most matter was neither gaseous, nor solid or fluid but existed in this fourth, superhot state. He tried to forget the body he was addressing. He was uncomfortable, but thinking of old Las, standing relaxed and spellbinding by the visualizer, made it easier. He had to tell these people that the solution was not to sit around. It was common knowledge that harnessed plasma possessed an extraordinary form of energy that would make it possible not just to shuttle to colonies in planetary orbits, but to emigrate for real.

"Plasma packs forces of hundreds of Mevs." The fact that no one interrupted him made him sweat, but it also gave him courage. The one he was afraid of was Soong Ast, but the colonist didn't pick up on anything he said. Professor Las had sketched plasma ships on the visualizer— long and fragile creatures of zero g. Last night he had dreamed about such ships, dreamed of sitting up front at the commands and seeing the hazy swarm of star clusters, like a giant mass of blue fireflies caught in midmotion and stilled forever. The thing was to get off this rock on the rim of the galaxy.

A faint smile seemed to play on the colonist's lips and Patel plunged ahead. Like Las, he asked questions. Sending migrating ships to where? Unlocking the innermost sanctum of matter meant you could send Noah's arks to Barnard's Star, which had many planets, and to 70 Ophiuchi, a triple star, one of which was very much like the sun. "The components within the proton and the neutron are the building blocks of the universe. It's just a matter of rearranging a few neutrons and protons and we have the strength of sidereal proportions."

He was about to get into quarks when laughter exploded on his left. It was Zeke Dua. For a moment, the Amcan delegate tried to control it, then threw himself back in his chair to let the laughter shake him senseless. Across the horseshoe, Iyabo Att and the Muscovite smiled politely.

Patel was confused. What was so funny?

"I'm sorry," Dua managed.

"The laughter before illumination?" Tok teased.

It took Zeke another minute of huffing and blowing his nose to calm down. Patel wanted to go on and get it over with, but the chairman held up a hand.

"I'm sorry but it's just wonderful," Dua chuckled. "I mean here we are and half the answer comes from a UN guard who has just been allowed to join the human race." He started to giggle again. "I'm sorry . . . I don't know your name . . ."

"Nobu—Patel Nobu."

"Nobu . . ." Zeke looked around for moral support but the others seemed embarrassed.

"What do you mean by half the answer?" the colonist asked coolly.

"The old sci-fi optimism," Dua answered, trying to collect himself.

"And what's wrong with that?" Soong asked.

"We need immediate answers." Dua turned back toward Nobu. "You're too far ahead of us,

kid. We're looking for new answers all right, but
short-term answers. We always are."

"Is free energy from colonist powersats also
too far ahead for you?" Soong asked.

Patel grinned. Soong Ast was on his side after
all.

"Are you thinking of turning them off?" Dua
asked point blank.

"I was thinking that a couple of hundred years
ago power satellites were also sci-fi pipe-
dreams."

"But you *could*, if we didn't behave down
here."

"It has never occurred to us."

"If we didn't vote for gericide, for example."
Dua looked straight across at Soong.

"Our destinies are interlocked."

"But for how long?"

Soong smiled. "You don't like sci-fi optimism."

Patel thought he could help the colonist.
"Plasma will deliver large ships to distant
targets . . ."

"The question is how we get from here to
there," Zeke cut in. The veiled threat of colonist
energy blackmail was out in the open and Dua
was digging in for answers. Looking directly at
Soong, he said there were earthsiders who didn't
particularly like the race of fractional humans
who were living in their fractional tin cans, but
there were also colonists who called earth a
museum piece and behaved toward earthsiders
with the condescension that premordials had
used toward their pets. How *did* the twin cylinders see the future? And, please, none of the

we-must-become-citizens-of-the-universe hom-
ilies. What were the council's long term plans?

"More colonies," Soong said calmly.

"And then?"

"A planet's surface obviously isn't the only
place people can prosper," Soong said. "And as
Nobu here says, when humans go to the stars, we
will go in large groups and be prepared to stay."

Patel seized the cue. "Plasma arks will lift off a
million emigrants a day." With a thrill, he
realized he had almost certainly won a berth on
the next ion ship out. This was his ticket. But did
Soong Ast actually know he was almost one of
them?

"I spent two years on a torus, second in command on a utility tug," he said quickly. "And as
soon as I have enough credits I want to apply for
permanent residence."

He looked for support from Soong, but it was
Zeke Dua who spoke. "I believe we're straying."

The UNCTAD delegate came to his rescue.
Looking up at him without hostility, she said
that the question was indeed how to get from
here to there. She was curious to know, she
added, what he thought they should do in the
meantime.

He should shut up, he knew it. But he said they
should of course keep the numbers in check.

"You mean you'd recommend gericide?" Sort
asked.

"Why not?"

"Would you say that being for or against
gericide is a question of age?" Sort asked.

"Maybe." He should have kept his big mouth
shut.

"But you realize that you, too, will be sixty,"

the chairman asked, glancing sideways up at him with a penetrating stare.

"Who wants to be that old—earthside?" As soon as he had said it, he was sorry. He wanted to be the chairman's friend.

Tok Sort was back again. "Would you work in a Population Care center, you know, pulling the lever to release the cyanide pellet, or whatever, if it came to that?"

"Wouldn't you?" He wasn't that dumb. "You'd have to live up to your own law, too, wouldn't you?"

"Got you there," Sal Belem winked to Tok. The Brazil delegate leaned forward and added they'd all have to be able to pull the trigger—he nodded toward the laser on the edge of the chairman's desk.

"People in charge have more responsibility," Nobu said. It was fun talking back to the delegates.

The UNCTAD lady looked up with a lopsided smile.

Tok Sort kept after him. "If we were one too many in here—like on a liferaft—would you execute the bingo player? I mean, if we were in a lifeboat like that and we flipped a coin, would you push the loser overboard?"

"That's unfair, Tok," the UNCTAD delegate said.

"Why?" Dua asked.

"You don't have to answer, kid," Belem told him.

But he answered anyway—to impress the colonist. "We've had emergencies, stacking mirror cells. A guy in an EVA pressure suit blew to pieces." It was only seconds after it had hap-

pened that he and Vassily had realized what
they'd seen. "It was the spin axis."

"Can you imagine nine technicians on EVA
missions repairing meteorite punctures on your
colony hull . . ."

"We call 'em blisters."

". . . and you coming with your utility vessel
to pick them up and, for some reason, it's the
wrong craft and only holds eight."

Nobu could imagine that since he had done it
many times, retrofiring as he approached blister
welders and pulling them in by their tethers,
their voices thin over the cabin speaker.

Sort rephrased his question. "If the nine of us
were on a raft and the raft would sink unless one
of us hopped overboard or was pushed overboard, would you do the shoving?"

"Why don't you answer your question yourself," the general said, looking sharply at Sort.

"Of course I would," said the Eurocom delegate.

"Even if it was Iyabo you'd have to push?" the
chairman asked Sort.

7

Tok felt the sting but kept his composure,
looking from Jammu to Iyabo and back again.
What did the chairman know?

He stalled. "You mean in this case, women
and children *last*?"

"Would you shove Iyabo overboard, I asked?"
Jammu's face was inscrutable.

The guard looked almost miffed at no longer
being the center of interest. Tok looked across
the horseshoe at Iyabo and smiled. He had to
raise the stakes. "Iyabo means a lot to me,
Jammu," he said, holding her gaze.

"I should hope so," she smiled back.

"And so do you, Jammu," he retreated. "And
so do you Zeke, and you Soong." He ended the
sweep of his hand on Sal on his right. "If we were
all on the eight-passenger raft in the middle of
the ocean, we'd all be precious to each other. But
if the raft would sink unless one of us went
overboard, we'd all become the possible
executioner of that ninth person. That's what I
mean." He looked penetratingly at the chairman
and felt Iyabo's eyes on himself.

"Such a corny example," Zeke sighed.

"Yeah?" he exploded. "Isn't that what colonist bingo is all about? Isn't it that we're too
many on this little hunk of solar satellite of
ours?" He was coming on too strong and in a
softer voice added that he would appreciate a
minimum of intellectual honesty. "What do you
say, Soong?"

The colonist hunched his shoulders as if to say
it was all self-evident. "A minimum of intellectual honesty, maybe combined with a sense of
urgency," he said.

"If you were one of the nine on the raft,
Soong," Tok insisted, "would you push the loser
overboard?"

Soong looked across at him. "If you put it that
way—yes," he answered softly. "I would also

expect to be pushed overboard if I were the loser.''

"And you, Zeke?"

"I don't buy your oversimplification."

"And you, Nobu?"

The guard grinned. "I'd push especially hard if you were the loser, sir."

"Why's that?" Tok asked icily.

"Because you invented the game."

"In the middle of the ocean it wouldn't be a game." The kid was getting cocky. He had thought of that when he decided to include the guard and the secretary, but he had also expected surprises.

"And you, Sal?"

"We all would," the Brazilian answered curtly.

"Bo?"

"I don't know," Bo answered apologetically. "I'd try to build a bigger lifeboat."

"That's evading the issue."

"I realize that."

Tok looked at the secretary, sitting so inconspicuously below the chairman and Patel Nobu.

She blushed and in a low voice mumbled that she could only say she was much too small to push anyone.

"Nice answer," Zeke smiled, making her blush again.

"I'm not even sure I know what a lifeboat is," she said.

"Your name is . . ."

"Ter Ki."

"In video classics, Ter," he said, "you must have seen people abandoning sailing ships."

"In classics, people are usually saved."

"Here, too, *most* of us will come off scot free."

"All Tallulah Bankhead loses in *Lifeboat* is her typewriter."

He smiled. The classic had been on channel 13 last week. "Her jewelry, too, no?"

"They use her diamond bracelet as fish bait when they're starving."

"Iyabo?"

She looked across at him with a mischievous expression. "I'd push you overboard and tie you to the side," she answered. "You could lie there bobbing in the water with a couple of lifebelts around you until the rescue hover showed up."

"Touché," he grinned with an expansive bow in her direction.

"Like that, all of us could tell our grandchildren about this crazy Tok Sort we once knew who nearly drowned in his own logic."

"Grandchildren?" he smiled.

"You have children, don't you? So does Bo, I believe."

"Two girls," Bo confirmed.

Iyabo kept her gaze on Tok. "Sal, Soong and Nobu and I and our videofan secretary are still entitled."

Ter blushed again.

Iyabo went on. "All Ter Ki and I have to worry about is getting pregnant before we're sixty. That's what Dr. Ast here suggests."

Tok felt she was egging him on and he loved it. "I hope that means my congratulations are premature."

She smiled. "A quota is something between a woman and her Population Care center."

"Not to talk about the woman's mate."

"If he's man enough—yes." She looked across at him without batting an eye.

The chairman cut in with a sharp little rap of his gavel. "If you want to know whether I'd push one of us overboard so the rest of us could survive, I'd say yes—if for no other reason than to expedite this debate," Jammu said, looking significantly from Iyabo to Tok. "I imagine that what you're driving at is that we're all, under the right—or wrong—circumstances, murderers."

Tok was certain Jammu knew, but he was also sure Iyabo hadn't told the chairman. He got up and put a hand on his wastepaper basket. "The idea is adopted then, 6-0, with the secretary, Bo Lim and Zeke Dua abstaining, or refusing to vote."

"Refusing to play, let's say," Zeke smiled condescendingly.

Tok put the other hand on the waste basket, lifted it up and gently shook it to shuffle the nine paper balls on the bottom. He put it in front of Sal on his right. "All we have to find out is *who*?"

"Who what?" Sal asked. "Victim or executioner."

The confusion was interesting. "Victim, I thought," he answered. "The responsibility for pulling the trigger will be collective."

"As always," Zeke said sarcastically.

Tok decided that after Belem, he would pass the waste basket around the other way so Zeke would be the last.

They all looked at the metal container in front of Belem.

8

Soong felt an urge to walk out, to get up and leave this increasingly premordial trap. This wasn't even a Delphic poll that would tell them what they expected of themselves. It was a descent into fatalism, a submission to fate. It was like a gravitational warp sucking them into a whirlpool of false solidarity, knotted guilt and bruised egos. But Zeke had stayed—at gunpoint. To think Jammu Nagpur would sear anyone to subatomic particles with the laser was silly, but the incident with Zeke at the door showed how scared the chairman was of the world outside. Yet they would soon face it—and be held accountable. And to raise questions and then argue that such questions weren't really relevant was no defense.

"We'll circulate this improvised urn here," Tok said, motioning counterclockwise toward Bo Lim on his left.

Around him, Soong could sense the need for going through with it. The straw poll was an atavistic urge to designate the sacrificial lamb, to be able to point a finger at a loser in their midst. Even Zeke watched the waste basket in front of the general with aloof disdain that couldn't quite mask his fascination. The urge to prove a point could be profoundly primeval and hostile.

"Ah, the hope of winning," Belem said looking into the waste basket. "Before homogenization, fate was also a sign of a primitive dislike of all forms of rational order—a perversity that made Southcone people instinctively unpunctual and temperamentally unorganizable."

"Napoleon said chance is the providence of adventurers," Tok smiled encouragingly to the general.

Belem dipped in. "Faith is, by definition, a leap," he said. His left hand came up with a crumpled paper ball and his face was frozen in a forced smile. After passing the container back to the hovering Tok, he unfolded the scratch sheet. "It says 'Yes,' " he announced.

"There are eight 'yesses' and one 'no,' " Tok smiled, "but I think we should keep them secret until we've all played." He shook the container and nimbly fished out a ballot for himself. "More fun that way."

"Except that you now know mine," Sal said, putting his ballot on his desk, face up, and smoothing it out so they could all see Tok's hand-scrawled "Yes."

"Just reduces the suspense by, what—eleven per cent," Tok calculated.

"And raises the stakes for the rest of us correspondingly," Bo said.

Tok put his own crunched paper ball in front of him while Belem leaned back, satisfied and ready to enjoy the others facing the odds.

"One 'yes' down, seven to go, and one nasty 'no'," Tok announced, rubbing his hands in mock glee.

Soong couldn't help thinking that war made people resourceful in a cunning, primal way and that inhabitants of Belem's system had mortgaged the psyche of several generations to the civil war whose beginning was lost in the

mist of the last century. When he was a little boy
his mother had taken him to the viewport sometimes, when their orbit was at its perigee, so he
could see the blue-white golfball they came
from. Once when the faint green contours of the
continents were visible above the southern
icecap, she had told him that people in the
South American cone were fighting each other
as on premordial video. And she had told him
that changing position on the earth's surface carried enormous implications and consequences.
To earthsiders everything became relative to
where they were. In school, he had found it difficult to understand the motives and sen-
sibilities behind the Southcone conflict, but to
look across at Sal suggested that the war had
been a clash of wills between resourceful people
who for some reason had narrowed their own
fields of options and hadn't known how to
synthesize social pressure. It could happen to
anyone without UICs. The impulse to prove a
point could run away with people, especially
people without ultraintelligence. Sal had told
him that you didn't have terminals in the jungle,
and that warfare was like passing kilo-
meterstones; it only marked stages along the
road. Older earthsiders still resented the colonists for not sharing the planetary guilt toward
the Southcone once the war was over. The twin
cylinders had seen no reason for "humanitarian
gestures" that would, in effect, reward murder,
underdevelopment and singularity. He remembered teachers being shocked at planetary insis-
tence that it was somehow okay for the ravaged
ecosystem to shoot part of its postwar problem to
the colonies in the form of excess migration.

"Pin not your hope on another's sleeve," Tok grinned as he passed the unwieldy urn to Bo.

Soong realized he would be next. To show both solidarity and distance, he decided he would pick a ballot and open it, but not show it.

Playfully, Bo closed his eyes and dipped into the waste basket. "Do you often play like this?" he asked.

"Decisions are sometimes more interesting in what they reveal than in what they solve," Jammu said with gravity.

Southcone immigrants had to be re-homogenized more than others, but they made marvelous settlers. They liked to develop new social forms and to take advantage of unparalleled opportunities.

Bo came up with a paper ball, opened his eyes and placed the ballot on his desk in front of him as Tok had done.

The eyes shifted to Soong.

"My brother-in-law says you play a lot of games in space—boredom, confinement," Bo said as he lifted the container up and placed it in front of Soong.

"Yeah, the long twilight." Zeke tried to make his voice sarcastic.

"What *do* you do on a Saturday night?" Tok chimed in.

It was Patel Nobu who answered. "Everything in a colony serves several purposes," he said. "Kids use tugs for sightseeing and cruising and inside the torus they 'dragonfly' over low-g swimming pools."

"But what do the fortunate colonists do who face no sanitation and still have a century to live?" Zeke asked.

"They ponder life's mysteries," Tok mocked, "while watching the leftover starlight from a future universe."

Soong could feel they wanted him to be the loser. Looking at Zeke, he said that to suggest that longevity meant boredom was the same as suggesting some genetic defect in people, some inability to flesh out their time with anything but the most annoying trivia. "You might just as well say that the experiences of people like us who aren't at least a hundred and sixty are pretty irrelevant since our imaginations are so cripplingly shortlived."

"You mean people like us just don't know what the hell we're talking about," Belem asked.

"When it comes to the vistas of extreme old age, no."

"Aren't you on the wrong side of your own argument?" Iyabo asked.

"How can a demand for food-to-population balance be a wrong argument?" Soong answered. "I agree extreme old age is a new frontier, but as Unido says, the planet will soon face deficit nutritional spending. Life is no candy store, the due bills are coming in. I'm sorry, but to me it's all quite simple." To emphasize his point, he tipped the waste basket toward him and looked down.

"To murder a third of all people over sixty isn't exactly trivial," Iyabo observed coolly. "You must forgive us a slight sense of malaise."

Soong picked the crumpled paper ballot in the lower left corner on the metallic bottom and passed the container to Iyabo. "If there's a malaise, I think it's because the exciting vistas of the future are not yet part of the planetary debate." He opened the paper ball, unfolding it with deliberate care, but the moment he saw Tok's handwritten "Yes," he shielded it with his hands and looked up. His eyes met Zeke's.

"What's so exciting about living in a tin can half a million kilometers toward Alpha Centauri?" Zeke asked.

"Being part of the future," Nobu answered.

Soong looked up at the guard and told himself he would have to deal with this technopol who so obviously was pitching for preferential emigration. But the argument was powerful. "Yes," he answered Zeke, "what would you say if one morning we discovered we were a failed experiment."

"To live in tin cans doesn't prove the contrary," Iyabo said.

"History must mean that our reach outward will continue."

"We may still be a fossilized dead end experience."

"True." He sensed she expressed the irritation surrounding him. "But shouldn't you be the first one to agree that natural selection has produced brains and intelligences increasingly competent to deal with the laws of nature?"

"Biologically, evolution is a series of improbable states," she answered, putting her hands on the waste basket.

Belem squinted across at him, but Zeke's eyes shifted to Iyabo. It occurred to Soong that Nobu and he were the same age. "Maybe intelligence and its integrity are the only significant opening to tomorrow. Young people usually have that sense of the future. They're tired of old arguments and looking for new frontiers."

But the focus of attention was on Iyabo, who wrinkled her nose mischievously and looked from Tok to the bottom of the container and back again. To dip in, she held her flowing sleeve.

"I wouldn't be surprised if there are several noes," she smiled. "Tok is such a cheat."

Tok smiled back, devastatingly.

Iyabo kept her ballot between her long hands.

Nobu went behind the chairman to Iyabo's side and lifted the waste basket from her desk toward the secretary. Ter Ki stood up to get hers and Nobu held it toward Zeke.

"I think I'll pass, if you don't mind," the Amcan delegate said.

"Are you getting too old to play games?" Tok smiled.

As Nobu reached into the container, Tok opened his own ballot.

9

Tok's own handwritten "No" stared back at him from his unfolded paper rectangle.

"You can spare the chairman the indignity," he told Nobu with a forced smile. "I'm the loser myself." He held up the paper with the "No."

Zeke grinned. "And you claim there's no God. I call that divine justice."

He would have to go on, Tok told himself. He felt his heart beat. It was dumb. If someone else had lost, he would have stopped here, probably with some last quip. Now, he had to go on. Men had died before in traps of their own making. He didn't believe it, but he couldn't stop at this point. Imagination was not essentially connected with images. In talking, words suggested other words and a person with sufficient verbal associations might be carried along for a long time. Words were becoming treacherous now, but he continued.

"How do we throw Tok overboard?" Belem asked good-humoredly.

"How about out the window?" Zeke joined in.

Words suggested other words and Tok said, "What's wrong with the laser?'

They looked at the weapon on the chairman's desk.

Zeke's smile was forced. "It is beginning to be amusing."

Tok's mind exploded with possibilities. He could see it happen and he could see it not happen. It was like when you were sent down to the principal for punishment as a kid. A minute before you had been like the others; now you had been singled out. Now, you couldn't unravel what you had been caught doing. He could see it happen and not happen, as if time could be turned backwards to just a minute ago. He could see himself as a shriveled lump of seared flesh and the others standing over him as over the victim of a ground car accident, shaking their heads in polite disbelief. Accidents were always stupid—or they wouldn't be accidental. A second, a minute ago you sat with your loved one in the cozy interior. Now she was lying motionless in a pool of blood and her trembling lips were the only sign of life.

He looked over at Iyabo, who was all seriousness now and understood what he was thinking. Her glance penetrated his. But he had done it himself. And life was cheap when it existed in twenty-two billion copies. His mind sought a way out that was not a retreat. He knew it all too well—the room, the horseshoe, the others. Yes, he wanted to go further, to rattle and shake convictions, his own included; to probe the darker corners of their collective imaginings. He had invented his little psychodrama to wipe the ponderous rectitude off Zeke's face although he loved him, to get under Sal Belem's studied toughness, to unmask Lim's smugness and Soong's robotized superiority, to inflict a wound on Iyabo's diffuse tenderness. "You didn't think I was proposing nine-player bingo just for the fun of it?" he heard himself say.

"Yes you did!" Zeke shot back. "You believed somebody else would lose so you could lecture us on the relativity of good and evil, or the opposing visions of good. It was a cheap shot, Tok!"

The vehemence surprised him. "Isn't suicide the only really serious question?"

"Sure, why go on living in a meaningless universe?" Zeke jeered.

How did you get off a verbal rollercoaster? "Then what are we waiting for? We have an executioner, a laser, and a democratically-designated loser and we have it all on tape for later if anybody feels a need to clear his conscience."

"And who's the executioner, pray?" Zeke asked archly.

"Nobu. He says he'll be delighted since I invented the game. Besides, he presumably knows

how to use a laser." He looked up at the guard.
"You can even vote him the authority to carry
out the committee's decision so he'll be off the
hook, personally." Perhaps imagination was the
absence of belief together with a shuffling of all
known elements.

"You are trying to provoke us," Zeke said.

"Yes, I am," he shouted, exasperated.

Jammu interceded gently. "Truth is often in
doubts, in humiliation, in what exceeds us."

Tok realized the chairman was trying to save
him.

"Maybe wisdom can have no center," Jammu
continued. "Maybe power, too, is elsewhere."

Tok felt he had lived forever, that he could
stand up and be seared into subatomic particles.
He thought of Kikki and the children. They, too,
would be bystanders at the cremation, innocent
and non-involved and taking their cues from
others. Kikki didn't deserve that. An accident
was an accident because those involved didn't
have the prescience to see it coming. A person's
involvement was with the self.

When Zeke spoke, his voice was subdued,
almost tender. "It's terrible to realize how little
acting has to do with real death."

Tok remembered Zeke was a doctor and
melted a little. He wanted to say he wasn't fak-
ing, that he *could* see himself as a dusty mote
floating in the void. He'd be sorry for himself,
but he could conceive it. Not that his death
would be a solution. "Why can't we be syn-
chronized," he wondered aloud.

"Why do we set ourselves up?" Belem asked.

"Do we?"

"Don't we?" The general's gaze was penetrating.

"The gambler's instinct, maybe."

"A gambler knows what to keep and what to throw away."

Tok felt the big Brazilian was looking right through him.

"A gambler knows when to hold on to his cards and when to fold."

Tok realized Sal also wanted to save him, but the way Sal looked through him almost challenged him to raise the stakes—against his better judgment. That, too, Sal realized, he was sure. "Why do we collide and intersect so helplessly?" he asked.

"We haven't had much practice maybe," Sal answered.

"Oh, I don't know," Jammu cut in. "I sometimes believe as many as six impossible things before breakfast."

Tok knew that Jammu understood, but also that Jammu was steering things back down toward banality.

"The important thing is to be free from habit," the chairman added.

Tok thought life was a banal accident in an indifferent universe, that man had already received his answers in the principles of evolution. You lived for the sake of living, for the things you were free to accomplish. He summoned up enough courage to look across at Iyabo.

"And what do we tell them down the hall?" Zeke asked in a voice that sounded benevolent.

"The truth." Tok was angry again. "You show

them the smoking remains and you play back the tape. It's going to bring the message home. UNISAVE FOR GERICIDE. UNISAVE STARTS AT THE TOP!"

"The funny thing is he's right there," Sal said, pushing his chair back and stretching his long legs toward Jammu's podium.

"REFORM BEGINS AT HOME," Tok declaimed. He couldn't help inventing other scanlines which he didn't articulate. Tok Sort first Bingo Loser. Sort Does It To Self. Guard Mercyslays Loser Sort. Death was that, he thought, a long tube whose end you couldn't imagine and whose beginning was forgotten.

"It is getting late," Bo Lim said quietly.

"Precisely," Tok said sharply. "We've been a little abstract about life up to now."

"Isn't it you who are abstract about life?" Iyabo asked.

He met her mocking eyes. "Individual life is pretty cheap, my own included."

She held his gaze. "I don't necessarily mean your life."

The illumination came in an exhilarating flash. The quota would be legit, if she could present *his* death certificate to her Population Care center. His first impulse was to dash around to her side and hug her, but he stayed where he was, shamelessly savoring the idea, and concentrating on ways to let her know. It was a frightfully powerful weapon, but she would give in and have the abortion if he had Nobu put the laser to his temple, if it was his life against that of the six-week-old fetus. Or would she? Motherhood was a deep instinct, the survival of the species and all that. His idea was ruthless and unfair and he was astonished at the audacity of his feverish mind.

"Ready, Nobu?" he asked without taking his eyes from Iyabo.

He sensed the guard snap to and imagined him looking to the chairman for his next cue. "Jammu says we must transcend our individuality."

"I want a vote before I do anything." Nobu's voice was gravelly.

Tok looked up at the guard and was met by a sullen stare. The guy might actually do it if ordered to.

"For the log," Nobu added, apparently realizing he was ahead of events.

Tok wanted to get back to Iyabo, but the guard was a distraction. Tok almost felt sorry for the kid—the kid? Nobu was no more than six, seven years younger than himself. And Nobu so desperately wanted to be back piloting his utility tug, to train for a deep probe. New ships were scheduled to set out for Alpha Centauri and Barnard's Star from the twin cylinders next year and Nobu had the stubborn humanism of true probers, strict and pure, austere and self-evident. But maybe Nobu's readiness to execute deadly orders had jeopardized his chances with Soong.

Tok decided he had to find out—before he died, he told himself. "I think my colleagues are too cowardly to give you the vote you're asking for," he told the guard. Then he turned to Soong and said he hoped the colonies would know how to reward loyalty.

Soong looked across at him with loathing.

"Isn't the sense of duty one of the prime qualifications?" Tok asked with put-on naivete.

"Together with an acute sense of judgment," Soong said coolly.

"Symbiotic judgment. We all know what we're playing for." He pushed on, saying he was sure Nobu would do anything to be part of a crew, to sit at the controls and feel the surge of the onboard computers lifting the crew's intelligence by the power of a thousand while their ship fell into orbit around a brand-new planet.

"Just like someone else we know will do anything to hold center stage one minute longer," Iyabo said seriously.

He looked across at her. "You're right. My exit must be swift and clean. Ready, Nobu?"

"Tok!" There was genuine fear in Iyabo's voice.

But he never got to tell her the terrible truth that his death plus her quota's birth still equaled zero and legitimacy because Sal Belem suddenly sprang from his chair, leaped forward and upward and lunged for the laser. The general's big body slammed against the side of the chairman's podium; he tripped and went down, bracing himself with his right shoulder and ending the slide on his knees.

"Sal!" Iyabo cried out.

Tok was on his feet.

But Sal came up again, with the laser in his left hand.

Across the horseshoe, Soong threw himself sideways toward Bo in a primitive reflex.

Sal unlocked the safety catch with a sharp click, pointed the laser at Nobu and backtracked.

Nobu just stood there looking silly. Ter Ki was shaking and Lim looked frightened too. Zeke

was in shooting range for a long second as Sal
moved backwards past him to his own seat.

"The meeting is yours, Mr. Chairman," Sal
said, sitting down with an enigmatic grin. He
put the laser down in front of him, carefully
without locking the safety catch. The barrel
pointed toward Soong's seat across the horseshoe.

Soong looked flustered as he sat up again.

Jammu folded his long hands over his eyes
and took over. He began with a prosaic recap of
the proposal before the committee, the amendment on the floor and the demand, already carried, for an overnight Arbitron. His voice was
soft and kind as he said they couldn't live with
suspicious minds, but that they would have to
hammer out a statement for the media.

Iyabo interrupted him. "But I thought you said
it was all futile, that the sun was running down."

She *was* loyal.

10

Chairman Nagpur kept talking while telling
himself they had failed Sort. Tok had been ready
to explore the essence, the mad and the dangerous. He himself had wanted to go further, but
lack of imagination stopped them. Was their
Unisave the ultimate symbol of pedestrian pro-
bity? It hurt to think so. Were they themselves
part of the problem instead of the solution?

Jammu tried to sum up in broad sweeps. The question before them was whether geriatric sanitation was necessary in the face of the projected collision between the ascending population curve, due to ever-increasing longevity, and the already maximized and therefore straight line of food production or whether the planet could get by with such optimistic measures as voluntary delaying of quotamaking in some workable form. Metapolls showed planetary division over the issue which meant the issue was being grappled with. And *that* in turn, meant public opinion didn't think the problem was insoluble. Goodwill came from trying to solve an issue, not from any vain hope of its solution.

"No phenomenon is a phenomenon, physicists say, until it is observed," he continued. The large human family was clearly observing the phenomenon of living for centuries since a large portion was ready to accept new limits to themselves, as seven years ago they had accepted the basic premise of Unisave, namely that unlimited fertility could no longer be considered a basic human right. It might therefore be said that the question facing the seven of them was whether they should institute mass murder on a scale that imposed new reverence for the birth-death equilibrium or whether gericide could be watered down to exemplary slaughter, to a ritual reminder of the balance between food and flesh.

"As always, we're wandering between a past that is no more and a future we can't really see yet," he added. "Another possibility is that we're asking the wrong question . . ."

"I agree," Tok interrupted. "Why don't we

admit that the one-person-one-child rule was our big thing. Why don't we go home?"

"Good idea," Iyabo said with an impatient gesture.

"I don't mean to adjourn," Tok said. "I mean to dissolve the committee, to vote Unisave out of existence. Our mission was accomplished seven years ago with the each-human-replacing-himself-only-rule."

"But it clearly isn't enough," Jammu said patiently.

Tok yawned. "Why must all noble ideas end as bureaucracy?"

Jammu felt they were edging toward the brink again. "Perhaps the question must be put a bit differently. Bo Lim here indicated the question could be stood on its head." He wanted to keep the debate going. Words were soothing and he wanted the Muscovite and the colonist to join in. Bo seemed resigned to sit through an argument that didn't concern him and Soong looked absent-minded as if he were already elsewhere in the solar system.

"Okay, Jammu," Tok said, "stand gericide on its head for us."

"Simple," he smiled. "If people will be living forever, there'll be no need for children at all—logically."

To let the idea sink in, he looked from face to face, letting his glance wander from Sal to Iyabo. Bo looked up.

"Come again," Zeke said, squinting his eyes as if he suspected the enormity of the proposition.

"Well, if we're going to be a superrace living hundreds and hundreds, perhaps thousands of years, our rate of replacement is going to be infinitesimal."

Soong looked up sharply. "But even Bo's voluntary abstention rests on the bedrock of gericide," he said. "Birthrates and deathrates *are* interconnected, symbiotically."

"Sure, but go one step further," he smiled to the colonist. "Tok's liferaft made me think that our basic premise, the one-to-one ratio, may be the big mistake."

"I'm sorry, but I don't follow you," Soong said. "I thought that Tok had demonstrated, in his own offensive way, that people will push their own kind overboard if it means saving the majority."

Jammu saw that Iyabo had understood, but he also became aware of the guard next to him. Why didn't the boy go back to the door? "You must make the effort and dissociate pediatrics and geriatrics and, above all, the one-to-one lockstep.

As he moved his eyes from Soong, he became aware that the laser was still in Sal's possession.

11

Iyabo felt instinctively what the chairman meant. "That means the end of absolute equality," she said.

"Only if you mean the right to reproduce is absolute," Jammu answered.

"It's the first law of Unisave, the right of everyone to replace himself or herself."

"Inevitably, if we start living hundred of years . . ."

"God, Jammu, do you realize what you're saying?" she interrupted, glancing toward Tok and the others for support.

But the chairman was recapping his idea. If longevity was the new fact of the approaching century, they might just as well vote themselves out of existence because their present mandate of overseeing the one-to-one ratio of human replacement would be obsolete. Within the next twenty to fifty years, people would no doubt begin to live for centuries—they might indeed be the first generation of quarter "millenniairs" themselves—and reproduction would inevitably reflect this new fact. Back in the twentieth century, rapid population growth broke down ingrained attitudes in long-settled communities of people living off the land. With village populations doubling every thirty years, people's integrated design for living lost coherence, causing mass migration, social alienation, rising violence and political upheaval. The only comfort to such runaway demographics was that high fertility was matched by high mortality. A century later, the deathrates declined so spectacularly, however, that we reached twenty billion and it was only during the last hundred years before Unisave that the planet reached birth-death equilibrium. Now, it was the other way around and if the equilibrium was to be maintained, the birthrate would have to plummet in direct proportion to the skyrocketing longevity.

Iyabo listened with growing incredulity. The chairman loved long, hypnotic monologues. She could feel he was struggling for order, for structure and that he was trying to legitimize the excesses of the last hours, but she also felt that only a childless person could come up with this kind of logic.

"I don't know if anyone is still interested in facts," she interrupted, "but biology sees life as a hereditary system, and sex and reproduction, birth and death, as means of transmitting heredity. Old texts say, 'Be fruitful and multiply,' as if to multiply is a consequence of being fruitful. The saying should go, 'Multiply and multiply and you can't help ending up a little more fruitful, a little more intelligent as species and as individuals'."

"Meaning?" Jammu asked.

"Meaning your superrace won't be very smart."

"You mean because they won't multiply fast enough?" Tok came in.

"If generations only replace themselves once every two hundred and fifty years, the rate of molecular transmission will be pretty slow."

"Really?" Tok smiled. "People living that long will presumably still reproduce in their youth."

She looked across at him. This was a new twist in the tug-of-war over their quota and she told herself Tok shouldn't win this argument. "They may reproduce in their early years, but the number of quotas will be one every two hundred and fifty years. That's four generations per millennium!"

"Guess there won't be much use for nurseries in the next century," Tok conceded.

"Chance alone is responsible for innovation." She remembered she had told him all this the first afternoon in his apartment. She had looked across at him and said that evolution was based on rare events and errors, but, unlike ground car mishaps, biological accidents were usually constructive. He had been sweet and unpredictable that afternoon. What had made her surrender was also the way he had made her feel that you could be lonely in a crowd. He had painted himself and her as solitary figures in need of each other's understanding. "No organism can go on producing exact replicas of itself," she added, "or we'd still be wallowing in the primeval ooze."

"Sexy," Tok hummed unashamedly.

But Soong turned toward her and said that what she was saying then was that gericide was biologically justified.

The colonist's seriousness jolted her for a second. "I'm not saying you should terminate life," she answered, "but biologically death is a necessity—yes."

"To evolve we must continue the turnover."

"The codes transmitted from generation to generation in DNA spirals favor cohesion, moral peace and aggressiveness."

But Jammu gaveled lightly. Homo sapiens was several billion years removed from the primeval ooze and Unisave's mandate didn't extend to evolution, he said. If, over the next million years, man slowed his replacement rate to four per millennium, it was hardly their responsibility.

"I'm merely objecting to your cavalier attitude toward the unborn, Jammu," she said, realizing she was on the edge of saying too much.

The chairman looked penetratingly down on

her. "The unborn or the unconceived?" he asked.

The chairman held her eyes in a vise and she knew he knew. But he backed off gently, saying their mandate couldn't possibly extend to those who were not yet. The proposal on the floor, he continued, was whether to mandate a draw among all sixty-year-olds in view of eliminating one-third of all persons over sixty so as to stabilize the planetary population at an absolute twenty-two billion.

She was confused. Something inside her wanted to defy Jammu's vision of a twenty-third century that had no need for children, no need for new life. But the future couldn't be fought with hypothetical beings, with those who were not here. Jammu was right there. A minute ago, she had wanted to have the quota in defiance, in an act of solidarity with the bustling of cellular life, but now she also realized that children shouldn't be had in anger. A quota was its own entity.

She listened to Ter Ki quoting from Soong's proposal. "Upon reaching the age of sixty, every man and woman will be compelled to take part in a draw. One out of three draws is negative and he or she will be eliminated by his or her local Population Care board."

The girl's voice was reverent. "He or she therefore has a two-to-one chance of going on living and enjoying the awesome benefits of modern science . . ."

"Thank you," Jammu interrupted, putting down his own transcript.

Ter looked up. A second later, Iyabo heard the metallic whine of the tape rewind.

They were back to square one and Iyabo told herself she could trust the chairman. She looked across at Tok, who was solemn and had his eyes on Jammu. Was Tok her friend? Last night he had said "no regrets," but also that he had to think of self-preservation. Fatherhood was not experienced in the flesh, but he should be her friend. He was not without courage. His psychodrama had also helped to bring them to this moment. But facing down the laser had aged him, made him look tired. She wanted him. She wanted him as he was, frayed and imaginative. She thought of Tunde. In a minute, Jammu would get to the end of the parliamentary rope and ask for a vote and all she could think of was her late husband's approbation. If he were there, he would rotate his chair and face her three-quarter profile—ALS victims had their vanity too, he used to say—and slowly say that she was a big girl now. But would he approve? She could see him sitting there with his nearsighted squint and ghost of a stoic smile. People had said his age was impossible to tell. The disease gradually destroyed the voluntary nervous system and the muscles but it left its victims youthful. Toward the end, he had pecked out a message for her: Remain earthy and essential. When she told him "earthy" had little meaning, he asked his terminal for synonyms and pointed excitedly to "realistic" and "unaffected" on the screen. She had held his thin shivering hand for a long while.

She looked up at the chairman. The quota would also be Tunde's, not in chromosomes—his vanity wasn't in cell nuclei—but in the essence of who she was. Single parenthood was giving more of your own substance, more of the sum of who you were. Jammu and Bo were going over the Moscom amendment. The quota was also a revenge on Tunde's amyotropic nerve cells.

"We can take an advisory opinion vote," Jammu said.

Bo had his nose in his folder.

"A nonbinding motion, that is," Jammu added.

"Fine. I withdraw then for redrafting," Bo said. "That'll also allow me to submit it for bioethics evaluation."

She could see Bo was happy again, absorbed, involved and plotting his next moves.

"Which leaves us the main proposal," Jammu said.

She was ready. She could only vote for life, for the mystery of the circumstances that, billions of years ago, led to the first molecule that could reproduce itself. Why did it occur just then? To understand that Tunde had devoted his existence. They had been called UNCTAD's first Pierre and Marie Curie in Stockholm, but she had never been in doubt that her prize was riding piggyback on Tunde's genius. He had been something of a misogynist when they met but his smile, at once grave and young, inspired confidence and he was later to say he had been fascinated by her because, instead of flirting, she had discussed nucleotide and rhodium atoms.

"All right, let's have it then," Jammu said leaning forward and nodding toward Ter below him.

The secretary began to read the preamble. The long courtship was conducted in strictly scientific decorum. His first gift was a desktop model of rhodium atoms in carbonyl clusters, and their honeymoon was spent attending the Tokyo biomass convention.

She noticed that her crumpled paper ball was still in front of her. She idly picked it up while listening to Ter. She would keep it, a memento of the four-hundred-and-whatever session. Tok's only yes.

She looked across at him. He was tense and impatient. She was glad that Tunde and Tok had met last summer at Montauk. It closed the circle. She hadn't known then that she and Tok would become lovers; he was there with Kikki and his youngsters, and she with her dying husband. It reminded her of what Jammu had said one evening out there. If you wish to know the road up the mountain, you must ask the man who goes back and forth on it. How could she have known then that there were any heights to climb. She had tried to talk to Jammu on the phone one night, but he had discouraged confessions.

Tok was listening, as they all were. She played with the paper ball and looked across at him. Something in his facial expression changed suddenly. He had that air he unconsciously displayed when he was on to something.

12

Soong listened to the secretary's reading of his motion of seven weeks ago with spent emotions.

Now they were there. In his mind's instant playback it was all worth it because they were there. This was it. He felt responses, feelings, ambiguities and passions fade within him. What was the point? In a minute they'd vote, and who had said what to whom was already fading into its own inconsequence. It was like traveling. Once your craft slid into the docking port and you heard the friendly swoosh of the airlocks, the trip was forgotten.

The secretary's voice made him think of Zad and his mother. Zad would be the first to know. She was still in the office—the others, too, no doubt—and they would call home together. His mother would hear it on the retransmission, maybe the visiphone of him giving the twin cylinders the news. Whichever way the vote went it would be behind him, and, to a large extent, behind the colonies, too. They had been invited to help solve a planetary problem. They had offered a solution. Earthsiders would have to live with the consequences. He couldn't think of any more evasions. The advisory opinion vote the chairman would allow on the Moscom amendment was just that. Jammu Nagpur knew how to be charitable without hurting the person he was kind to. They would vote and the laser staring across at him from General Belem's desk would be returned to the guard, whose status upgrading he might look into when he got to the twin cylinders. Previous experience, motivation and group response were the prime criteria for immigration. Initiative was rarer in beehive recruits.

Next to him, Iyabo Att played with her unopened paper ballot, rolling it between her long fingers. He couldn't help watching. Yes, they played a lot of games—yes, boredom and confinement sometimes—but not with the craving to risk death which seemed to be the latest earthside perversion. Human perversion, he corrected himself mentally. There was something very wonderful in winning when the stake was your life. To risk and to win. Maybe he would mate with Zad Gran and settle on one of the experimental rim habitats. It would be refreshing to be with people establishing their ideals in new cities and new meadow sections, to be part of high synergy dynamics, to be part of a felicitous imagination. A doctor was always welcome and both Zad and he knew social forms and practices here. Settlers tended to think of the planet as chaotic, but the two of them knew it was not all entropy.

Ter was at the resolution itself, reading in her melodious Hundred-Forty federation accent. "Upon reaching the age of sixty . . ."

It occurred to him that they would vote on what he had just called a perversion, that gericide was institutionalized life-gambling. But it would also be a tonic. You rolled the dice and when you survived, you walked away invigorated and energized. You had tested your nerve and you had won your life.

He felt Tok's eyes were on him. Was he thinking the same thing? Why had the colonies come up with a crap game to stabilize population? Soong couldn't answer that one now, but his mind formulated hypotheses all by itself. Weren't the colonies themselves a gamble to show mankind wasn't a failed experiment? Was it something subliminal in colonists? He felt himself wanting to swallow. He shifted in his seat and let his eyes wander past Bo to Tok Sort.

Their eyes met.

Soong thought he saw a trace of irony in Tok's face, and he was certain Tok was reading his mind. Any native-born colonist like himself would think of himself as a winner. But in a cosmic sense, it could of course be said that the dice were still rolling.

". . . and thereby stabilize population figures at absolute zero," the secretary finished.

The colonies were way stations to the stars of course. The drift through space was just beginning. The guard might go and his descendants might see Alpha Centauri become a glowing new sun and its planets more than nameless asteroids and begin colonizing a new star system.

Jammu was solemn, but his handsome features betrayed no emotions as he spoke. "Will those in favor of the proposal on the floor . . ."

"Excuse me," Tok interrupted. "But how about floating odds."

PART V

1

Zeke Dua felt the suck of the gravitic elevator taking him down to ground level. He was both wide-awake and dead tired. He leaned against the back of the empty elevator and damned himself for having taken the last quaracin. This was the third night like this. He had wanted to ride home with Tok for a relaxing postmortem—Tok was good at giving things comic relief—but Tok had said he and Iyabo were going for a soothing drink. He had invited himself along and the three of them had repaired to Tok's apartment building penthouse.

Tok and Iyabo were still up there.

He felt the elevator decelerate. He was sure the others were all sprawled out in deep, exhausted sleep, overcome by fatigue and release. Maybe not Jammu—he couldn't imagine the chairman asleep in anything but a spare, chaste position. Before the drinks, it had been Lan and Dal Hoo. "The President is most anxious to hear it first hand," Lan had insisted dramatically as they fought their way into the office through the newshounds who wanted more than the statement Jammu was reading in the committeeroom. He had downed the quaracin in his private waterroom in the middle of the office pandemonium and before Hoo got on the line. The President had been happy—visibly happy on the visiphone. Yes, Dal, gericide has been avoided.

Yes, although it will be suspended over everybody's head if absolute, or negative, growth isn't achieved. Yes, a kind of standing-the-colonists'-proposal-on-its-head compromise which, in essense, means that young people who want children will play bingo instead of sexagenarians. Couples wanting offspring will go to local Population Care boards for a lottery. One draw in thirty will be denied conception.

The elevator doors slid open and he crossed the hallway, past the apartment nameplates and entrance scanners. Lan and the others had watched the conversation on visiplates. No Dal, it wasn't our scenario that swung anything; we could have spared our efforts in Berkeley and this morning over breakfast.

He passed through the glass doors and got into his UN ground car.

"Home," he told the driver.

The chauffeur punched the direction into the dashboard and dutifully lowered the volume of a radio playing soft night music.

"No, leave it," he said.

As the car slid into the uptown traffic and found its own luminous track, he told himself that Tina would be sleeping now. Of course she had seen it on video, but he should have called. It had all been so hectic—until the three of them had found refuge in 'Tok's rooftop restaurant. The President had pumped him for details, but he hadn't said much. Residual solidarity—or the residual guilt of poker players who had almost gone too far—he was sure the others wouldn't say much either. As it stood, Dal, it was the Moscom amendment for do-it-yourself abstention that broke the logjam. The idea was to shift the responsibility for over-sixty life from Unisave, PC boards and municipal systems to the individual, meaning that you personally guaranteed the continued existence of your over-sixty relatives. But it had floundered because there's obviously a limit to how long a woman can delay childbearing. Yes Dal, the breakthrough had come much, much later, after debate on means of divorcing fertility and longevity and all sorts of things. Very exhausting.

He hadn't told the President about the floating odds—one in thirty for now, one in twenty-five next year maybe. Their subcommittees would compute fertility statistics very carefully. As Bo Lim said once Tok had sprung his eleventh hour surprise, the new rule would either spur everybody on to fulfill their quota or it would make young people even more lethargic and cause a plunge in birthrates. The breakthrough had come at 0015 and they had faced the bedlam in the hallway at 0130.

As always, traffic was heavy in the uptown tunnel. He couldn't help but marvel at the simplicity of their original rule. One to one. It had been so simple and, as it had turned out, so easy to administer. If the Amcan system had a 3,220,556,776 population in 2188, it would have no more than 3,220,556,776 in 2198 or 3018. Now, things would be messier. Soong had suggested one-in-thirty as a condition for his support and they had let it stand at that until the demographics could be finetuned. How long would it take before demographers would realize the numbers could be manipulated? Maybe everybody should be told what the floating odds were at all times. Maybe they should issue bulletins on the monthly lottery odds, or have UICs calculate them, so anybody with a pocket calculator could doublecheck the ratio of probability.

The car resurfaced at Ninety-fourth Street. Old mistrust might come back otherwise. Lottery boxes in outlying, unconditioned areas might be stuffed with too many noes. Or people in left-behind regions might *suspect* there were more noes in their lottery boxes than in those going to capital beehives. Why hadn't it occurred to him earlier?

Because he was tired. But why did it occur to him now that he was even more tired? Another sign of precocious senescence? He had skipped the more depressing chapters in Berkeley, but some morbid curiosity had made him ask more questions, about endocrinal secretions causing sexual atrophy. Sexual senescence didn't always bring about the extinction of the libido. He liked the euphemism and imagined hundred and eighty-year-old satyrs flogged along by lust and red-hot instincts.

The car decelerated at the old armory on Ninety-fifth and swung west for the last fifty meters. The radio brought a news summary, read by a throaty feminine voice. The first metapolls were being started in the Hundred-Forty federation and most other eastern hemisphere systems on Unisave's new baby bingo. Before voting with the others, he had made a last stab at absolute equality. Maybe it was the physician in him, but he couldn't help believing that a twenty-year-old was no more anything than a hundred and twenty-year-old. On an emotional level people felt it was a tragedy to see a child die in a hospital bed while an old man in the next bed pulled through. The argument for the child was that it hadn't lived, but a child's future was always hypothetical whereas the hundred and twenty years of the hundred and twenty-year-old were real. A dying Beethoven had composed nine symphonies, a dying five-year-old—what? His reason was specious, he admitted, because there were hundred and twenty-year-olds who had never accomplished anything. But then again there were no guarantees that the five-year-old would ever do anything. Accomplishments sounded hollow in an operating room. There, all flesh was equal.

"Good night," he said getting out of the car.

"Sir."

In intensive care it became a little different again, a little more emotional because you subconsciously pulled harder for the kid. It seemed a bigger victory. He entered his building and passed the scanners. But the kid's survival was not at the expense of the patient next to him. Children were more loveable than seniors, but that was all right. Loveable children didn't take the breath away from their elders.

He got into the elevator and punched his floor. He couldn't help thinking that when facing death all life was equal. And if life was equal then everybody should play colonist bingo, one-year-olds as well as hundred and one-year-olds. Why hadn't he thought of that earlier?

He'd remember that one if gericide came up again. In the meantime, however, it was baby bingo. All of Unisave was going beddie-bye now, except himself—and Tok and Iyabo up there at the penthouse restaurant. It was ridiculous. At least they wouldn't meet until Tuesday. It had been Jammu's idea after they drafted the statement. Shamelessly, they had voted, 7-0, for a four-day weekend. Even the little secretary had smiled as she recorded the vote.

He punched his door combination and pushed the door open as quietly as he could.

"Zeke?"

"Honey." He stopped tiptoeing and crossed the apartment to the bedroom. He peeked in. Tina was sitting up in the bed with cream on her face. The wallscreen was on but the audio turned down.

"Where have you been?" she asked, stressing the syllables in the way he knew all too well.

"I'm bushed, hon," he smiled, coming into the room.

"You sure look it."

He could afford to be expansive. "Well, we did it," he said, crossing to the dresser and putting down his attaché case. "Humanity can go beddie-bye or upsie-daisie or whatever. Gericide is out."

"Yes, congratulations." She looked up and forced herself to smile. "The Fems called, a few other friends too."

He couldn't help using the chance to fib. "Yes, I tried to call. You were busy."

"You're a hero, Zeke."

He unzipped his uniform front. "To unwind, Tok and Iyabo and I adjourned to the penthouse restaurant in his building. Nice view."

"She looked ravishing in her UNCTAD garb." Tina flipped off the video and settled down in the bed.

It occurred to him that Iyabo had never told them why she was wearing UNCTAD robes. He could still see her walking the long way around the horseshoe and simply asking Sal to give the laser to her, then handing it back to the guard. The boy had put the weapon back in his holster and made them all feel miserable. Iyabo had said a kind word, and Soong had promised to look into a possible upgrading of the boy's immigration status.

"Anyway, no session till Tuesday," he sighed. It was when the guard had walked back to the door that he had realized they would survive it all, that institutions had their own dead weight and that people had it, too. The guard was not the only one to integrate his assigned role. They had all become their usual selves. It was so easy to slip back into what you were.

"Remember what I told you this morning?" Tina asked.

His mind was blank and he looked at her for a hint.

"This morning," she smiled intriguingly.

Then he remembered. "Yes, I asked everybody. The play on the tenth."

"That's not what I mean."

He walked into the waterroom. He was too tired for a shower and just slipped out of his uniform. Maybe he and Tina should have a child. During his residency they had talked about it. Maybe there was more to reproduction than seminal expulsion and ovarian cycles, more than demographics or ZG. What was it that the bearded kid had said in Royce Hall the other night? The mystery of procreation.

He got into his pajamas thinking about the

days on the Oregon coast. Everything in them should have rejected the conditioned expanse, but Tina had looked for driftwood and they had sat together and looked at the sunset. Perhaps it was all in the eye of the beholder, perhaps reality was in your veins.

When he came back into the bedroom, Tina had dimmed the light and stretched out.

He got into bed on his side. "What did you mean?" he yawned. It felt great to lie down.

"Oh Zeke."

But her voice was not impatient. Then he remembered and smiled in the darkness. "You mean about me in the White House last night. No, I'm not having an affair with Iyabo."

"Not you, silly; Tok is."

2

"Surprised?" Bo asked.

Misha Sev's face broke into a smile on the screen. "No, you said you'd call."

"A little later than I'd expected." He saw it was already morning in her living room.

"Perfect time for me."

Now that he had her on the other end of the line, he realized he didn't know her that well, that he wasn't sure he wanted to tell her everything.

"I also promised your former colleagues I'd call," he began. "They all extend their best wishes, Sal Belem, Zeke Dua . . ."

"Thank you, I saw them on the news," she

interrupted. "I saw all of you coming out there. Congratulations."

He couldn't help asking her what she thought.

She took her time. "You've abandoned the one-to-one."

"Gone off the gold standard. That's how Tok Sort put it."

"He would say that, wouldn't he."

"But wasn't it bound to happen sooner or later. I mean, if we all start living hundreds of years. . . . That, incidentally, was the chairman's final argument."

"The end of an era." Her voice was noncommittal.

Somehow it was important for him that she approve. In a few long phrases he explained how no one would have to be sanitized, just fewer people would be born, very few people fewer. He added that, gold standards or not, true synergy had been achieved, but he didn't tell her that their baby bingo unanimity had come after Iyabo had disarmed Sal.

"That's what the Today Show said, unanimity."

"How would you have voted?" he asked.

She hesitated. "No one will have to be sanitized, as you say. I guess there were no other options. I mean I trust you exhausted them all."

"We did."

"I thought I understood you . . ."

"The first inkling came when Sort suggested decreeing lower-than-zero birthrates, which led to a discussion of the right to live vs. the right to reproduce."

"But before that, didn't you . . ."

"An amendment."

"You told me about new research in nitrogen fixing and superplants."

He tried to read her face and could only see dogged innocence. He was torn between wanting to know what she knew and wanting to avoid letting her know he had been used.

"No, our proposal had nothing to do with bioengineering," he said. Then he plunged ahead and told her. He wanted to know if she would spot the flaw immediately and told her what had been in the manila folder. He told her that over-sixty losers of colonist bingo would escape sanitation if their children postponed having a family.

She smiled approvingly and he became devious enough to add that the reaction had been joyous. Zeke had suggested that people without offpsring be exempt from bingo playing altogether and Iyabo had been the first to say this was something she could vote for.

"Lo Hals?" she asked.

"Lo Hals and a whole braintrust."

"And?"

He held her gaze on the screen. "Weren't you part of the input?" he asked gravely.

"No, but I wish I had been," she smiled.

He felt out of it. Her open, trusting face said she wasn't lying but he couldn't totally believe it. Why didn't she see through it? To force her, he repeated the basic premise of the amendment and went a little further, saying a bingo loser could go on living as long as his or her descendant of quotabearing age postponed having a child. "On a one-to-one ratio, one sixty-year-old minus one nonborn grandchild equals zero, obviously."

"I can imagine they liked it," she nodded.

"But?"

A shadow crossed her face. "But what?"

"Well, a woman can't wait too, too long, can she? Soong says the present state of the art puts sixty-five as the cutoff for successful and safe pregnancies."

She smiled again. "So?"

"So, if a bingo loser wants to live a full life to a hundred and sixty, say, his or her daughter will never get around to having a child since by then she'll be a hundred and thirty herself." He was beginning to be a little irritated.

"I realize that."

"So, it doesn't work."

"You told me about superplants being eight, ten years down the road the other day."

"A little less, actually."

"So, the children of bingo losers wait, what, six, seven years before they have children of their own. It's a wonderful short-term solution. I think you and Lo Hals are just brilliant."

For Bo, the rest of the telephone conversation was subdued. He bravely kept up the front while his mind ran over his options. Should he resign and dash back to the anonymity of his lab at Bykov U or was this new humiliation a baptism of fire, a first lesson on the new job. The events of the past week had been turbulent. To sort things out maybe all he needed was a good night's sleep—a good *day's* sleep; it was 0312 local time.

"But anyway, you decided to go with baby bingo instead," she said.

"We did." He realized he was lucky. At least he had called Misha first. It would be much easier now to dial Lo Hals.

"I'm sure metapolls will ratify your decision. It's not perfect, but it's something people can live with. One-in-thirty, you say?"

"Floating odds, linked to absolute demographics, actually."

She nodded and continued talking while he told himself he would either stick with microorganic research or he'd mature into something else. Recombinant synthesis on a personal level. Maybe his own lupine root nodules were learning something.

Misha stopped herself and looked at him with an expression of affection and concern. "But you must be exhausted."

He answered with a wan smile. "We voted ourselves a long weekend."

Her smile said a lot about acceptance, about appeasement, accommodation and adjustment. When they hung up, he told himself he'd call the Duas over the weekend and see if he could meet Mrs. Dua and enlist her goodwill in his search for a nice apartment.

A minute later, he dialed Bykov U and asked for Lo Hals.

3

Tok slid his left arm under Iyabo's neck. He needed to hold her as their mating fever ebbed.

The darkness was warm and safe, as was her nakedness against his. His mind skittered around the edge of its own awareness, but there was nothing to think of, nothing to say. The only thing he became aware of after a while was the purr of the acclimatizer, and even that sounded soothing and placid.

He kissed her temple, softly and tenderly. He breathed deeply and smelled her hair with its redolent echo of perfume, of the long day and long evening behind them. His eyes were closed and their legs were still intertwined.

"A night together, finally," he whispered.

"Or what's left of one," she sighed, turning her head inward in his arm to nestle in the hollow of his shoulder.

His lips grazed her ear and with his left arm he hugged her tenderly and held her even tighter. She returned his caress by pressing her thighs around his.

He kissed the top of her head. "Why didn't I think of that before?" he smiled in the darkness.

"I like Zeke."

When they had left the committeeroom to face the music in the hallway, he had suggested that they at least sit in a quiet corner somewhere and have a drink. Somehow Zeke had been right behind them and invited himself along. A second later they had been engulfed by the newspeople but before that they had had time to exchange a glance that said they had both hit upon the idea simultaneously. The three of them passing his apartment scanners was innocence itself.

He moved his free hand down along her arm and across a chasm to her belly. Her skin was hot and moist. The rest had been a matter of sitting it out upstairs and, when Zeke looked at his digit and got up, ordering one last one. They hadn't been the only people in the restaurant. Technopols offered toasts and congratulations from other tables. When the two of them casually got up and walked to the elevators they took their time. He answered a guy who said he didn't agree while Iyabo signed a menu and went to a phone to punch a do-not-disturb code into her home number. He had done the same thing when they got down here. Even Kikki would understand that he'd be zonked out. It was uncanny how odiously clever you got to be.

He didn't want to think about the world beyond the acclimatizer. Not yet. The night —what was left of it—was protecting. And feminine. Maybe it was her clothes somewhere in the room, maybe it was the scent of her hair, an odor of evanescent perfume with a whiff of deeper musks. Solitude was to be savored.

"Sleepy?" she whispered.

"I guess so."

His eyes were closed but every nerve-ending of his system experienced the moment. He felt her left hand move from his chest and seek his face. Slowly, her index finger began to trace the contours of his features.

"It's good," he said. He meant her stroking. He meant the two of them, their ingenuity, their being together, love, the night and a lot of other things, but words were superfluous.

He thought of Soong getting ready to fly home. Soong had come out of his office with his mission chief as the three of them rendezvoused to go for the drink and had told them he was taking the first ion cruiser out this morning, but that he would be back Monday. Soong had invited them to come with him for the long weekend. Zeke had said he and Tina needed an earthy weekend, Iyabo had used the pretext of UNCTAD business, and he himself had mumbled something about giving the idea a raincheck. Maybe it was an idea although he couldn't see himself and Iyabo managing to get lost on a colony. Before heading for the auditorium roof elevator to catch a hover with his assistant, Soong had said the invitation would of course remain outstanding. What was her name? She had been at Montauk last summer with Soong, a second generation colonist who played a sharp game of tennis.

"You feel different," Iyabo whispered. "For the first time."

"How?"

Her finger had stopped at his lips. "Your skin, softer, different."

Gently, he bit her forefinger, to show her there could be no more agreeable meaning to things. He caressed her tummy with his right hand and his fingers touched the crown of her pubic hair. It was beautiful to drift away to sleep together.

She moved her hand to his chin and lay still.

His mind was beginning to drift but there was one knot that wouldn't melt. It lived and grew, deep under his right hand, the one in twenty-two billion that couldn't exist. Upstairs she had said that if she were a newly-married woman who had decapsulated and become pregnant, she might terminate her pregnancy since there was no longer anything to prove. Zeke had weighed the hypothesis as if she had asked for his physician's opinion. Would I advise a pregnant woman to terminate because baby bingo had become law? Zeke answered himself with a smile. If a woman was pregnant, she presumably would have played baby bingo and already drawn a yes.

His right hand traced an imaginary line to her navel. Her belly was beautiful. He had wanted to ask what she meant, but Zeke had proceeded to fertility statistics.

"Have you made up your mind," he asked.

Her answer took a long time. "Yes," she said, moving her hand away from his face.

It was the second time tonight he had had the feeling he had to go on despite himself. Again, he could see it happen—the child, the disgrace; and he could see it not happen.

"And what's your decision?" he asked.

She sighed in the darkness. "You ask too many questions."

"Maybe I do."

A long minute later, she said she would do what any sensible woman would do—have it terminated.

He was relieved. It was silly, but he had to know why. "Because there's no longer anything to prove?" he tried.

"No, because there's no reason to ruin our lives." Her voice had an edge of bitterness.

His arm was beginning to hurt but he didn't want to move it from under her head. "Do you think that's how most women will react to baby bingo?"

"I don't know, Tok." Her voice sounded tired. "I can only speak for myself and only for this particular instance."

He squeezed her gently, to show he respected

her and that he was grateful. There was no reason to ruin their lives.

She squeezed him back, kissed his temple and turned on her back.

This was the moment to say he would divorce Kikki, the moment to say he would have himself restricted and, once the scandal blew over, would apply for derestriction and perhaps conceive a legitimate child. But he didn't say anything. He thought of the quota growing inside her, cells dividing and subdividing at a prodigious rate. Life had nothing to do with legitimacy. Scientists no longer questioned life in test tubes, but analyzed systems of life, to see how it was "made" and how it evolved. Life was patterns and contingencies. He had to gamble one more time; he had to tell her that there was one solution. He wouldn't be able to live with himself if he didn't tell her.

"We'd be something—you and I and the halfquota," he said, smiling at the idea. "And celebrity has its own crazy logic. We'd be so famous, so infamous, we might be allowed to emigrate to a rim habitat."

He had said it. He could see the two of them and the child tucked away in the torus of a colony, the planet's two biggest cheats finishing out the elongated old age together with their grown offspring. Poor kid. To be the son or the daughter of the two of them and always looking hurtfully at life.

"Don't worry, I'll do it," she said.

But his mind was still on their hypothetical life as a trio. Mom and Dad and innocent victim. "It's just that as solutions become harder, it's

more difficult to decide which answers to eliminate."

"I know," she sighed.

"What I mean is that it isn't that simple for me
either."

He could feel her turn her face toward him on
his arm. He looked into her dark eyes and barely
visible face. She was beautiful.

"Can you sleep?" she asked.

"Yes." He was wide awake. It was silly to be
too excited about sleeping together not to be able
to fall asleep. Pattern and contingencies and
when to decide to drop alternatives. Everybody
regrouped facts. Everybody elaborated probable
structures and expressed conclusions in pru-
dent, neutral terms. Why hadn't their ancestors a
few centuries ago realized that too many people
meant paralysis and metadetermination instead
of absolutes. Baby bingo also trivialized life,
made it manageable and reasonable. The absolute of sanitation was avoided but life became
floating odds. Or maybe it had always been like
that.

It was the prospect of his own execution that
had given him the idea of baby bingo, his death
that would make the quota legitimate for Iyabo.
Minus one plus one equals zero. Was it his playing with his own absolute that had made Iyabo
get up and walk the long way around the horseshoe, past Soong, past Bo and himself, to ask Sal
to give her the laser. It had been a tense moment.
Sal rose until he towered over her, a tapering line
in his uniform facing her robed wholeness. He
handed her the weapon while pointing the barrel toward his own chest. Magnificent Sal. She
must have understood the gesture because when

she in turn gave the laser to Patel Nobu, she also held it toward herself as if to deprive him of the weapon. Mind over matter?

She reached up with her right hand and removed his arm from under her neck. He kept her hand in his as their arms came to rest between them. Man had chosen mind over matter long ago, but no one could abstract himself from his fellows. Food and people would bisect in ten years. The colonies had been right in bringing it to everybody's attention. Unisave concerned itself with the growth and evolution of the planet by concerning itself with the affairs of the individual. And the system was best served when individuals weren't given maximum freedom to do whatever they wished. Such freedom was only possible when everybody was aware of constraints, when everybody realized it was impossible to own one another, to own progeny, land or knowledge. The whole earth perspective was in all people now, but that didn't mean they shouldn't exercise collective vigilance to keep pushing their systems toward seamless unity.

Iyabo turned toward him. He could feel her warm flank against his left side. To sleep together was forgiveness, one human being letting down all guards toward another. The way it worked for him was to lie flat on his back and hold the hands across the chest, like a stiff. He turned on his back, making Iyabo move. He was sure she was sleeping.

He folded his hands over his chest and felt their flanks touch. Iyabo said life wasn't so much one building block on top of another as a crucial permanence. After five minutes he would have the urge to roll over on the side. The trick was to resist. The urge would increase of course but so would the drowsiness. Man was still young in cosmic terms. In the time perspective of the universe, Iyabo and he were recent, tentative, perhaps even experimental.

Can't Find An Ace Science Fiction Title At Your Local Bookstore?

BOOK MAILING SERVICE can supply you with any Ace Book currently in stock. Just fill out the coupon on the facing page (or supply the information on a separate piece of paper if you don't want to rip out the page) and send it together with a check or money order made out to Book Mailing Service for the cover price of the books you order plus 50¢ each for the first three titles to cover postage and handling. After the first three, we absorb additional postage and handling charges: for three, six or one hundred books, postage and handling totals only $1.50 per order. (No postage and handling required if order is accompanied by <u>Destinies</u> subscription.) This offer is subject to withdrawal or change without notice.

And remember—the Editor of <u>Destinies</u> is also the Executive Editor of Ace Science Fiction. On the following page you will find a list of current and recent ('78/'79) Ace sf titles that he feels will be of special interest to the readers of <u>Destinies</u>. (To order a catalog of all Ace Science Fiction titles currently in stock send 50¢ to Book Mailing Service, refundable on your first order.)

BOOK MAILING SERVICE
ACE SCIENCE FICTION DIVISION
BOX 650
ROCKVILLE CENTRE, NEW YORK 11571

Ace Science Fiction
Purchase Order

NAME _____

STREET _____

CITY OR TOWN_____

STATE & ZIP _____

Please send me the following:

COVER PRICE

TITLE _____

AUTHOR _____ _____

TITLE _____

AUTHOR _____ _____

TITLE _____

AUTHOR _____ _____

TITLE _____

AUTHOR _____ _____

TITLE _____

AUTHOR _____ _____

POSTAGE & HANDLING _____

TOTAL _____

Please enclose a check or money order made out to
BOOK MAILING SERVICE for the total of the cover
prices of the books ordered plus 50¢ per book for postage
and handling. (Maximum $1.50) No postage and han-
dling required if order is accompanied by <u>DESTINIES</u>
subscription.

The Book Mailing Service policy is to fill an order for any
title currently in stock upon receipt. However, delivery is
usually from one to four weeks since postal transit time
must be taken into account. Payments for titles not in stock
will be promptly refunded.

Current and Recent Ace Science Fiction Releases of Special Interest, As Selected by the Editor of _Destinies_

Poul Anderson, ENSIGN FLANDRY **$1.95**
FLANDRY OF TERRA **$1.95**
THE MAN WHO COUNTS **$1.95**
James Baen, THE BEST FROM GALAXY,
VOL. IV. **$1.95**
Donald R. Bensen, AND HAVING WRIT **$1.95**
Ben Bova, THE BEST FROM ANALOG **$2.25**
Arsen Darnay, THE KARMA AFFAIR **$2.25**
Gordon R. Dickson, PRO (illustrated) **$1.95**
David Drake, HAMMER'S SLAMMERS **$1.95**
Randall Garrett, MURDER AND MAGIC
(fantasy) **$1.95**
Harry Harrison, SKYFALL **$1.95**
Keith Laumer, RETIEF AT LARGE **$1.95**
RETIEF UNBOUND **$1.95**
Philip Francis Nowlan, ARMAGEDDON 2419 A.D.
(revised by Spider Robinson) **$1.95**
Jerry Pournelle, EXILES TO GLORY **$1.95**
Spider Robinson, CALLAHAN'S CROSSTIME
SALOON **$1.75**
Thomas J. Ryan, THE ADOLESCENCE OF P-1 **$2.25**
Fred Saberhagen, BERSERKER MAN **$1.95**
THE HOLMES/DRACULA FILE
(fantasy) **$1.95**
LOVE CONQUERS ALL **$1.95**
AN OLD FRIEND OF THE
FAMILY (fantasy) **$1.95**
THE ULTIMATE ENEMY **$1.95**
Dennis Schmidt, WAY-FARER **$1.75**
Bob Shaw, SHIP OF STRANGERS **$1.95**
VERTIGO **$1.95**
Charles Sheffield, SIGHT OF PROTEUS **$1.75**
Norman Spinrad, THE STAR-SPANGLED
FUTURE **$2.25**
G. Harry Stine, THE THIRD INDUSTRIAL
REVOLUTION (science fact) . . . **$2.25**
Ian Watson, MIRACLE VISITORS **$1.95**